Alyssa

LETTERS FROM WOLFIE

LETTERS
FROM
W☮LFIE

PATTI SHERLOCK

VIKING

VIKING
Published by Penguin Group
Penguin Young Readers Group 345 Hudson Street, New York, New York 10014, U.S.A.
Penguin Books Ltd, 80 Strand, London WC2R 0RL, England
Penguin Books Australia Ltd, 250 Camberwell Road, Camberwell, Victoria 3124, Australia
Penguin Books Canada Ltd, 10 Alcorn Avenue, Toronto, Ontario, Canada M4V 3B2
Penguin Books (N.Z.) Ltd, 182-190 Wairau Road, Auckland 10, New Zealand

First published in 2004 by Viking, a division of Penguin Young Readers Group.

3 5 7 9 10 8 6 4

LIBRARY OF CONGRESS CATALOGING-IN-PUBLICATION DATA
Sherlock, Patti.
Letters from Wolfie / by Patti Sherlock.
p. cm.
Summary: Certain that he is doing the right thing by donating his dog,
Wolfie, to the Army's scout program in Vietnam, thirteen-year-old Mark
begins to have second thoughts when the Army refuses to say
when and if Wolfie will ever return.
ISBN 0-670-03694-3 (Hardcover)
[1. Dogs—War use—Fiction. 2. Vietnamese Conflict, 1961-1975—Fiction.
3. Brothers—Fiction. 4. Emotional problems—Fiction.
5. People with disabilities—Fiction.] I. Title.
PZ7.S54517Let 2004
[Fic]—dc22
2003024316

Printed in U.S.A.
Set in Esprit
Book design by Kelley McIntyre

*I want to thank those
who gave me indispensable help:*

Charlotte Sheedy, my agent, who sent me a magazine article about war dogs and asked, "Is there a book in this?"

Ronna Marwil, my friend and walking buddy, who listened and encouraged with great patience.

Lt. Col. Mike Vorachek, Deputy Commander, 652nd Area Support Group, U.S. Army Reserve, who answered endless questions and read the final manuscript.

Dennis Aslett, Idaho Department of Fish and Game biologist, former marine and Vietnam veteran, who shared his Vietnam experiences.

Sgt. First Class–Retired Jesse S. Mendez, scout dog instructor at Fort Benning, Georgia, during the Vietnam conflict, who granted me lengthy phone interviews.

Dennis Sutton and Bob Baker, radio guys in the sixties and early seventies, who made a musical history of the evolving protest movement for me.

Burl Summers, sergeant and team leader, Third Battalion, 506th Infantry, 101st Airborne Division, who shared his Vietnam diaries.

Regina Hayes and Melanie Cecka, my editors, for their insights and enthusiasm.

Members of my writers' group: Mike Ingram, Debbie Empey, Dave Clark, Brian Cornett, Jamie Jonas and Linda Nelson, for feedback and nurturing.

And Shakespeare, my German shepherd mix, for providing the model for an extravagantly happy dog.

To Matt, Shane, and Mary, with love

1

I laid out Wolfie's things on the throw rug in my room: the silver choke collar, the worn-out red leash, his fancy dog brush, a bunch of toys. I had searched the house and yard that morning and collected a sackful of items so that I could decide which to send with him.

Wolfie sat beside me, his face level with mine. August sun coming in the window lit up the hairs around his face, giving him an uneven halo. He leaned close and his tongue snaked out. "No!" I said. The tongue retracted with a disappointed *sloooop*.

He smelled like grass and fur and dog biscuits. I put my arm around him. His tongue slurped my cheek. I was inconsistent; that's why I hadn't cured him of licking.

I stared at his big paw resting on my thigh.

"It's going to be harder to say good-bye to you than it was to Danny." Then I wished I hadn't said it. When your brother is a soldier in Vietnam, you don't want to jinx anything.

It's not like I don't miss Danny. Everybody does. When Danny's around, it's like he's the only person in the room.

My mom laughs at his jokes like he's the funniest guy on earth, and if Dad or I say, "Let us in on what's funny," those two raise their eyebrows and look at each other, and hardly ever cut us in.

I reached into the sack and pulled out a yellow sock toy. "Remember when you got this, boy?" Danny had given it to him at the birthday party my friend Rick and I gave when Wolfie turned a year old. That was two years ago when we were eleven, before Rick and I quit doing kid stuff.

Wolfie had been huge even then—not as tall as now, but his coat fuzzed out in a puppy way that made him rounder.

Wolfie reached out to take the sock in his mouth.

"No," I said, pulling it back. I wanted to keep sorting.

Wolfie's head sagged on his neck. He could be sad with his body, though his face had a permanent smile.

I rubbed his head. "When we're done."

I lifted out a small, frayed collar, the one Wolfie had worn home from the animal shelter when I first got him. For months, I had been stopping by the shelter on Saturdays, but the day I saw the litter that included Wolfie, I turned up the pressure on Mom and Dad.

I pulled out a blue Frisbee, but hid it from view with my body. It would torment Wolfie to see the Frisbee and not get to go play.

Wolfie leaned his considerable weight against my shoulder.

"Let me finish. Then we'll go pl—" I caught myself. If Wolfie heard the word *play*, he'd get so excited and demanding I wouldn't be able to finish what I was doing.

I pulled a rawhide chew from the sack and gave it to Wolfie. He dropped to his belly, turned his head to the side, and started gnawing it with his huge teeth.

2

I'd leave on him the red collar with the engraved plate that said, "Wolfie. I live with Mark Cantrell," and in smaller letters told our address and phone number. But the army would probably replace the collar with one of its own.

Danny had written us about the army's need for scout dogs as soon as he got to Vietnam. It was 1969 and the war was supposed to be winding down, but Danny said the army wanted to get more scout dogs over there and was trying to recruit them from civilians.

I stood up all at once, not wanting to sort anymore. Wolfie let the rawhide fall from his mouth. His ears snapped forward and he stared at me with his unmatched eyes. His one blue eye, along with his size, probably meant he had malamute in him, mixed with the German shepherd; that's what the animal shelter had thought, anyway.

I braced before speaking the words, "Want to go play?"

Wolfie sprang up. His paws skidded on the bare floor and he slid into the rug, scattering everything. Scrambling, toenails scraping the floor, he got back his balance and blasted out the bedroom door. I followed, carrying the chewed-up Frisbee and his leash.

Wolfie stood beside the front door, staring at it like that might make it open. I clipped the leash on him and reached for the doorknob, which wasn't easy because Wolfie took up a lot of room.

"Move," I said. He did, getting in my way more.

When I had hold of the knob, I said, "Easy." I didn't want him charging out the door and yanking me off the porch.

But that's what happened. He lunged into the bright sunshine. My feet left the porch, I hit the grass running, and we were off, tearing down the street.

Mom had bought me a choke collar a couple years

before because she worried Wolfie might pull me into the path of a car. I hardly used it anymore because Wolfie usually walked on a leash okay. Unless he was excited. Then it was "look out."

Near the entrance to the park, an old woman was walking a little white dog with red ribbons on its ears. The woman looked over, saw us, and flinched.

I stopped and made Wolfie sit. Barely. He was a rocket, ready to launch into the air.

I unclipped the leash. "Okay, boy."

The woman saw Wolfie was free, and moved in front of her dog to protect it. She was so thin and shriveled, I don't know what she could have done against a 110-pound elephant dog.

The little dog rocked back and forth, yapping. Wolfie gobbled up the ground to the woman and her dog. When he was a couple feet from them, he put on his brakes and skidded to a stop, as I knew he would. I'd seen him in these situations dozens of times before.

The women scolded, "Get out of here! Go away!"

Wolfie inched out his front paws and dropped his head onto them.

The woman asked me, "Is he friendly to other dogs?"

"Very."

She warned in a quavery voice, "If he touches a hair on Prince Valiant, I'll call the cops." To Wolfie she said, "Stay there, and I'll let Prince Valiant come say hello." She limped forward while the white dog strained against its leash, barking threats.

The white dog touched noses with Wolfie. Wolfie sat up. That made him tower above the other dog. The white dog curled its lip in a snarl. Wolfie looked down, his permanent smile in place.

"Your dog is very gentle," the old woman said. She leaned over and put out a gnarled hand.

Wolfie sat still as a statue while the woman's wrinkled fingers came down on his head.

"So big," the old woman said. "And so kind."

Usually when people spoke to him, Wolfie got delighted and pounced on them. But if the person was very old or very young, he somehow knew he needed to be calm.

"Look what nice manners this lummox has," the old lady said. After a minute, she withdrew her hand, still smiling at Wolfie.

I said, "Let's go." Wolfie walked a few careful steps away from the woman, then exploded into a run. I raced behind him to the middle of the park.

For the next half hour, I threw the blue Frisbee and Wolfie chased after it. He was a little clumsy on the jumping part—if he caught the Frisbee in midair, he'd land with a thud. Even so, he hardly ever missed.

Clouds moved in, shadows moved across the grass, and the air started to cool. Thunder rumbled, and the wind began to whine. I tucked the Frisbee into the waistband of my jeans, and clipped Wolfie's leash onto his collar.

"You'll play with Frisbees in Vietnam," I told him. "Danny says the handler he met throws Frisbees for his dog.

"Maybe you'll even see Danny." There actually wasn't much chance of that. I'd looked at a map of Vietnam, and it was a big country.

At home, I went back to sorting. One by one, I put the ruined toys in the wastebasket. The few good toys and the dog brush I put back into the sack.

It had been silly to think I might send Wolfie's things with him. The army would just throw them away.

5

Anyway, I didn't know how memory worked in dogs, if those toys would even mean anything to him when he was halfway across the world living with soldiers. I tried to imagine him there, moving through the jungle with guys carrying machine guns.

I put the sack on the floor of my closet. It would be easy to find there when memory acted up in me.

2

In June, before he left for Vietnam, I asked Danny if he was scared. I mean, guys were getting killed over there. He said, "No way, Marcus Aurelius. I'm going to be home before you know it."

"Mom says it will be over soon."

"It will be when Daniel the Ultimate Warrior makes the scene." He pounded his chest, gave an awful cry, and plowed into me. He lifted me up, making a Tarzan scream, and dragged me out the door into the front yard. The sprinkler was running.

Wolfie dashed to the middle of the yard and ran in a circle, excited to get in on the action.

"Danny Warrior meet nasty Vietcong—scare to death!" Danny deposited me on top of the sprinkler.

I yelled. My hair was dripping into my eyes, and I had a stripe of mud on my jeans.

I looked up, and Mom was standing in the doorway. "Mark," she said sadly, looking at my pants.

"Mom, *who* is going to keep this kid shaped up when I'm gone? Marcaroni, keep out of the water!"

"Go change your clothes, Mark; Danny has a plane to catch. And wipe that dog's feet before he comes in."

* * *

Driving to the airport, we got pretty quiet. I stared at the mountains in the distance; Dad searched the radio for classical music. I couldn't see Mom because I was sitting behind her. I figured she was trying not to cry.

Danny strummed an imaginary guitar. I watched him out of the corner of my eye. He had been out of high school a year now. He had gone to basic training in March, and when he came home on leave, his arms and shoulders had gotten huge. I wondered if I'd get muscles like that some day and quit being skinny. It wouldn't be bad to have Danny's face, either, though he wasn't as good-looking as before, when he had hair.

At an intersection where we stopped for a red light, three hippie guys sat on the curb smoking. All of them had shaggy hair and no shoes. One wore a bright purple tie-dyed shirt.

Dad grumbled, "Roll up the window so we don't get high."

Mom said, "Did you see that beautiful shirt?"

Danny flicked me on the arm. "Hear that, Markmallow? A Christmas hint. Mom wants a tie-dyed shirt to wear to PTA."

After we parked, I walked beside Mom to the terminal. I kept glancing at her. She had no expression at all.

A minute before Danny got ready to board the plane, Mom put her arm around his neck. She looked into the distance and said in a nonchalant way, "Write, Son." We laughed at that because Danny hardly ever writes letters. Mom used to nag him to write Christmas thank-yous, but even when she bought ready-made cards and all Danny had to do was write one sentence and sign his name, he'd still forget. Me, I get started on a thank-you, and before I know it, it's four or fives pages long and my hand is getting a cramp.

I was the next one to hug Danny, and I whispered, "I'll miss you, Peaches." He said, "I'll miss *you,* Tinker Bell."

Dad hugged Danny then, and got misty. He coughed and said, "We're proud of you, Son. Young men have served this country whenever . . ."

"Gotta go, Dad." Danny rolled his eyes at me. Dad was about to launch into a speech about people doing their duty. He's big on us boys doing our duty and serving in the military, but the Vietnam thing will be over before I'm old enough to enlist.

Danny picked up his duffel bag and started to walk off. Mom was gazing down the concourse and didn't seem part of our group anymore. Danny turned around and looked back just before he went through the boarding gate. Dad and I waved like crazy. Mom's hand fluttered about waist level and she looked into space, not at Danny.

As the plane taxied away, we stood there, not moving. I thought about Danny's grin, just before he disappeared through the door. Something wasn't right about it. It wasn't at all like the killer grin he'd flashed in his yearbook picture. Our neighbor Mrs. Heimbach says it's Danny's smile that makes girls find lame excuses to drop by our house. This time, Danny's smile was the kind a little dog makes when a big dog is sniffing it.

* * *

When Danny was in boot camp, Dad had expected

he'd write to us because the training is so hard and guys get lonely. But we only got one letter.

Dear Mom, Dad and Marcaroni,
Superglue. That's my personal solution for treating foot blisters. As you know, we march a million miles a week. I gave up on bandages, tape, and extra socks. I got the glue from a secretary in the main office (a big girl who looks like someone's 4-H project). I put the glue over the blister, and that protects it from rubbing. The other guys are trying it. We don't know what will happen when we try to get the glue off.
My favorite food here is 1) macaroni and plastic cheese, 2) oatmeal, nice and crusty from sitting in a vat for an hour.
Dad, you should have told me drill sergeants have no sense of humor. I missed chow last night because I had to scrub the latrine floor with a toothbrush. I would have starved if friends hadn't sneaked me brownies from the mess hall.
Love,
Danny

"Are those kids crazy?" Dad asked. "How will they get superglue off their feet?"

Mom said, "I wonder what sort of joke Danny played that got him in trouble?"

Dad grinned. "Probably nothing he'd dare write home about."

"Leave it to Danny to liven things up." Mom smiled.

Danny, Danny, Danny. Always the center of things wherever he was, even in boot camp.

* * *

Danny had been in Vietnam just a week when he wrote that the army was looking for German shepherds. A dog had saved seven guys in his platoon from an ambush. He didn't say any more about the ambush; I'm pretty sure he didn't want to worry Mom and Dad.

Dad asked, "What do you think, Mark?"

Mom stared at him. "You're not serious?"

Dad pointed at the page he'd been reading. "Danny says, 'Maybe Mark should send . . .'"

Mom frowned. "Danny just got there. He hardly has his feet under him."

I broke in. "No."

They looked at me.

"Wolfie's not going."

Mom's face relaxed.

Maybe the army needed dogs, but no way was I parting with Wolfie.

* * *

A couple days later, Rick and I were on our bikes when a car slowed down and a high-school girl with long red hair leaned out the passenger window.

"Mark!"

Rick lifted his brows. "Who's the great chick?"

The girl moved hair off her cheek and called, "How's your brother? What do you hear from him?"

"He's in Vietnam now."

Her face crumpled. She withdrew into the car without saying anything. The driver pulled away from the curb.

Rick said, "Girls really dig your brother."

"No kidding."

* * *

Next morning, Effie Heimbach was sweeping her walk when I came out on the porch. She called, "Mark!"

"Hi, Mrs. Heimbach." I bounced over to see her.

She put her hand on my shoulder. "Mark. How is your bruzzer?"

"Okay."

"This will be your job now, Mark. You must keep me up to date on Danny."

Something went out of my morning, like it had been punctured. I had thought that after Danny left, things would be different. But if anything, Danny was more popular than ever. When was it going to be my turn?

I was buying tomato soup at the store for Mom when Mr. Sevorn, who owns the grocery store, hurried toward me. He smiled. "What do we hear from my Danny, huh? What does he think of 'Nam?"

"He's muddy."

"I miss him, you know?" Danny used to work for Mr. Sevorn.

I stared at the soup display like it interested me.

"How about you, Mark? Got anything to brag about?"

I looked up, surprised.

Mr. Sevorn took off his glasses and cleaned them on his apron.

I don't know where the next words came from. "I'm thinking about sending my dog to Vietnam."

"Your big dog?"

"Yeah. They need dogs over there." I tried to sound casual.

"Mark!" He stared at me. "That would be a very heroic thing to do."

12

Mr. Sevorn said, "You hear that, Angie?" Gabrielle Burnett's big sister, who was stocking toothpaste, looked up. He repeated what I'd said.

"What's your dog's name?" Angie asked. She had huge brown eyes, like her sister. Gabrielle Burnett and Claire Richardson were the prettiest girls in my school.

"Wolfie."

"Wolfie the war dog," Angie said.

Mr. Sevorn grabbed my shoulder and gave it a painful squeeze, like he used to do with Danny. Then he looked past me. "Hey! I just heard the news!" he said to someone behind me.

I turned, and there stood Dad.

"What news?"

"About Mark sending his dog to the army."

Dad frowned in confusion.

"Randall, you gotta be proud. You got a pair of fine sons. Boys who are willing to make sacrifices for their country."

After I paid for the soup, I walked out with Dad.

"I didn't think you were going to send Wolfie."

"I'm just thinking about it." Truth was, I wasn't thinking about it. I couldn't face losing Wolfie.

But should I be thinking about it? Mr. Sevorn thought sending Wolfie was the right thing to do, and Angie thought it was cool.

"Want me to help you get more information?"

I looked off toward a faraway mountain. It couldn't hurt to get more information. "Okay."

Dad called the army and asked if donated dogs had to be purebred. The man said he'd check and call us back. A day later, he called back to say that purebred dogs were preferred, but the military needed dogs and would take a mixed breed into training, hoping it would

13

show the shepherd temperament and intelligence.

School was starting soon. If word got around about Wolfie, it might impress Angie's sister Gabrielle, or Claire Richardson.

"Wolfie would do fine," Dad told Mom at supper one night. "Look how fast Mark taught him to walk on his hind legs."

"If he's so smart," Mom said, "why can't he learn to quit jumping on people and knocking them over? He's so easily distracted, I don't see how he'd be much good as a military dog."

To me she said, "Mark, with Danny gone, wouldn't you be awfully lonely without Wolfie?"

"Eve, Mark is almost a man. Let him decide."

For the next couple of days, I walked around with a headache from thinking so much. When I thought about how it would feel to say good-bye to Wolfie, I'd have to put the subject out of my mind.

Then, listening to the radio one morning, I heard about a VC raid that had killed a dozen U.S. soldiers. Danny lived in danger, and instead of appreciating that, a lot of the time I just felt jealous over how much attention he got.

If I sent Wolfie, maybe I wouldn't feel so guilty.

I told Dad to call the army and tell them Wolfie would be their new recruit.

* * *

The weekend before school started, we delivered Wolfie to Fort Carson, Colorado, about seventy miles from our house. A storm moved in just after we left home, and by the time we got there, we'd been rained on twice.

We stopped at big metal gates with a sign, "Welcome to Fort Carson." It didn't look all that welcoming. A guy wear-

14

ing khakis, a black helmet with the letters MP on it, an armband, a whistle, and a gun came out of the guardhouse.

"May I help you?" the MP said. Dad reached out the window and shook the guard's hand. "Randall Cantrell, formerly of the First Cavalry."

"Where were you stationed, sir?" the guard asked. Just then, Wolfie poked his head out Dad's window, pushing Dad aside.

"Hi there, boy." The guard rubbed Wolfie's head with his knuckles. "Geez, friendly dog." I had thought the guard was old, twenty-five or thirty, but now I could see he was only eighteen or nineteen, like Danny.

"Wolfie. Get back!" Dad tried to push Wolfie into the back seat. That was useless; Wolfie was getting petted. "I played trumpet with the division band at—" Dad couldn't finish. Wolfie had almost shoved him out of his seat.

"Mark, help!" Dad ordered. Wolfie was hanging out of the car, front paws on the guy's arm, licking his face. The guy's helmet slid over one ear.

"Quit!" the guy said, laughing.

"He's going to be trained as a military dog," I said.

"Yeah?" The guard lifted his brows. He reined in a smile. "Okay."

He went to the guardhouse and phoned the officer who was waiting for us. He came back, told Dad how to get to the building, and scratched Wolfie behind the ears. "Cute dog," he said.

Dad drove the post's winding roads to a white building. A man in khakis with a lot of ribbons on his chest stood in front of the building, rigid as a phone pole. Next to him stood another guy in fatigues.

"You don't need to bug me about posture, Mom," I said. "The military will straighten me up." When I got to be

15

eighteen, I was going to join the air force. Dad had talked a lot to Danny and me about the free college education we could get by going in the service.

Mom turned around and looked at me with a solemn face, like she was about to say something big. But after a minute all she said was, "Roll up your window; it might start raining again."

I put a leash on Wolfie. The minute I did, he lunged at the door. His head bonked against the window.

Mom shook her head. "That dog."

"The window was open a minute ago." I petted Wolfie where he'd hit his head.

"He doesn't pay attention," she said.

"He's eager, Eve, not dumb," Dad said.

I hung on for dear life, but Wolfie dragged me across the lawn to where the men waited.

"I am Captain Forsythe." Everything about the captain looked freshly ironed: his hat, his shoes, his smile. The man shook hands with Dad and me, and Mom shyly moved behind Dad.

"This is Sergeant DiBello."

Dad shook hands with the sergeant.

"Here's our new recruit," the captain said.

The sergeant nodded at Wolfie.

That's all it took for Wolfie. He thought the sergeant liked him. Wolfie yanked the leash out of my hands and lunged. A second later, the sergeant had a wet-pawed dog all over him. "Down!" the sergeant commanded, giving Wolfie a knee in the chest.

Dad said, "Sorry" and "Bad dog!" The sergeant grabbed Wolfie's leash, brushed himself off and traded a look with the captain.

"Please come inside," the captain said, and opened the door to the white building.

"I'll stay here with Wolfie," I said, and noticed that my words creaked.

"Sergeant DiBello will stay with the dog. They will be here when you get back." The captain moved behind me and we all went into his office.

After we sat down, the captain put his smile back on and said, "The army is grateful to you, Mr. and Mrs. Cantrell, and especially to you, Mark, for making this sacrifice for our country. People like you, who are willing . . ."

I craned my head to see if I could see Wolfie. I could. A couple of soldiers had come across the lawn and were trying to get Wolfie to roughhouse with them. But Wolfie wouldn't play; he just stared at the building, his ears at attention.

"Any questions?" the captain asked.

"Will Wolfie have a year's tour in Vietnam, like my brother?"

The captain looked at a space above my head. "The army isn't very good about predicting the future." He stood up then, and we went back outside.

When Wolfie saw me, he bounced up and down on his hind legs, then dragged the sergeant across the lawn to the parking lot.

Mom knelt down on the pavement beside Wolfie and stroked his head.

"Wolfie, you be careful, boy," she said. "Don't go jumping up on people all the time. Don't eat anything plastic. Don't get into the trash and steal chicken bones. And don't act silly; you're going to be a soldier."

Then Mom, who hates to draw attention to herself

17

and hardly ever cries in front of people, dug her fingers into Wolfie's fur and started to bawl. I mean, loud enough that you could hear. She hadn't cried when we said good-bye to Danny, but she was sobbing over Wolfie.

The two soldiers who had been playing with Wolfie looked at Mom and lost their grins.

"Wolfie," Mom choked. "Wolfie."

Wolfie cocked his ears at her and put his nose into her face. Then he butted her in the chest in his big oaf way, and Mom toppled onto the pavement.

Danny would have loved to be at the center of a scene like that. He wouldn't have minded if Mom had gone into hysterics saying good-bye to him and had to be dragged away.

Dad helped Mom up, and Mom wiped her eyes.

Then it was my turn to say good-bye. My eyes got all wet, but seeing how Mom was taking it, I thought it'd be worse for her if she had to worry about me. So I held it in.

"Maybe Mom is right—maybe you'll wash out," I whispered to Wolfie. That would be a perfect outcome. I would have done an unselfish thing by sending him, but he wouldn't have to really go. No one would think any less of Wolfie for being too friendly to make the grade.

Mom and Dad were watching me, so I looked up and made a joke. "I told him to write."

Dad said, "We can probably expect as many letters from Wolfie as from Danny."

Dad was right in predicting we'd hardly get any letters from Danny. But soon after, I started getting regular ones from Wolfie.

3

The first letter really wasn't from Wolfie. It was about him.

Dear Mark,

I am pleased to report that your dog, Wolfie, arrived here at the scout dog training facility at Fort Benning, Georgia, in good health.

Dogs assigned to our program undergo a twelve-week training course. They are housed in roomy kennels, which are cleaned morning and night. We provide the dogs with fresh water at all times and a diet specially formulated for working animals.

Dogs and handlers trained here will lead patrols. Training begins with basic obedience commands, which are new for some dogs and review for others. Dogs learn to run obstacle courses, become accustomed to guns and hand grenades, detect ambushes and mines, and ride in helicopters.

On behalf of the United States Army, I want to

thank you for your generosity. Dogs have served our nation in important ways during two world wars and in the Korean conflict and are playing a critical role in Vietnam.

Yours truly,
Richard Lenz, Captain, U.S.A.
Public Affairs Officer,
Headquarters Detachment, Scout Dog Training

P.S. Enclosed please find a picture of the UH-1 Air Mobile Operations Iroquois helicopter, suitable for framing.

An eight-by-ten black-and-white photo fell out of the manila envelope. It showed a monstrous helicopter, black and gleaming.

"Cool." I showed it to Mom. "It's a Huey."

I shook out the envelope and turned over the letter. The back was blank.

"What are you looking for?" Mom asked.

"I thought there might be a picture of Wolfie or the place where he lives."

Mom took the letter and read it. She handed it back. "Well, he got there."

"I wished they'd said more about him," I said.

"It's a form letter they must send to everyone who donates a dog."

"But it says, 'Dear Mark,' and talks about Wolfie."

"They change the names for each letter."

"I want to know how he's doing in his training." I took the glass of milk Mom handed me. "What do you think they do to dogs they get mad at?"

"Cancel their weekend passes." Mom ducked her head,

like she does when she makes a joke. Then she looked thoughtful. "Now that you have the name of someone to contact, you could write and ask specific questions."

"You think they'll write back?"

She shrugged, pulling a spiral notebook from the kitchen drawer.

I didn't know whether to send my questions to the person who sent the form letter or to the handler who would be working with Wolfie, whose name I didn't even know. After a few minutes, I decided to write to Wolfie in care of Captain Lenz, the one who signed the letter. I meant to write a short letter, but by the time I got done asking everything I wanted to know, I'd written several pages and my thumb had a blister.

* * *

I was looking at the map of Vietnam that Dad had hung above the kitchen table. Dad came up beside me and gazed at it, too.

He pointed at various cities in South Vietnam. "They've infiltrated here, and here, and here." I knew who he meant by "they." The Communists.

He moved his finger over and pointed at Laos, then Cambodia, then Thailand. "You can see what could happen if we let them have Vietnam. They'll take over these countries next. Then what? Australia?"

It was depressing to think about. One country after another falling under Communism.

"We don't want to be fighting them someday in Hawaii," Dad said. "We have to stop them now."

* * *

"They target the dogs." Gene Dorweiller laid his head

21

back on the top of my desk so I was looking at his face upside down. His eyebrows were where his mouth should be and his mouth, looking toothless, was at the top of his face, opening and shutting.

Mr. Casey, our American History teacher, stopped writing on the board and let his hand hang in midair. He looked over his shoulder.

"My dad said the VC have a bounty on dogs. A buddy of his has a kid in Vietnam and told him," Dorweiller said. "If the VC shoot a dog, they get—"

"Dorweiller!" Mr. Casey snapped. "What is so important that it can't wait until after class?"

Dorweiller lifted his head off my desk and blinked. He turned his head slowly to the left, then to the right, eyes flickering. Girls started to giggle.

Dorweiller has a big head, pig eyes, and pale freckled skin, but chicks like him. Girls dig show-offs, I guess.

"I was telling Cantrell that VC soldiers get extra money for shooting dogs."

Mr. Casey scowled. "I don't see the relevance of that to the subject. You are aware of our present topic?"

Dorweiller lifted his eyebrows and made his eyes wide, as wide as pig eyes could go. "Uh, the Declaration of Independence?"

A wave of laughter rolled over the room.

"That was last week. We've moved on to the Revolutionary War."

"That's what made me think about Cantrell's dog. Talking about war." He bounced his head.

I stabbed Dorweiller in the back with my pencil. I never should have told him about Wolfie. I didn't want him blabbing it to the class. I didn't mind the idea of it getting out, but I wanted it to happen another way. I wanted to choose who knew about it. Like, I could have casually mentioned to Claire Richardson that I had a dog in training in the army. When she pressed me, I could have admitted that I had done an unselfish act. What I definitely didn't want was a class discussion about the actual dangers Wolfie might face.

"Mark, did you send a dog to Vietnam?" Mr. Casey asked. "I didn't know they were using dogs over there."

"He's not there yet. He's in training." I addressed this to the top of my desk.

Mr. Casey nodded. "That must be an interesting story. However, we don't discuss Vietnam in here." His words came out like bullets. He turned and started writing on the board again.

A hush hung over the room. If I'd been a mouthy guy, I would have asked why we didn't discuss Vietnam in an American History class, but I wasn't going to be the one to break the silence. Five minutes later, when the bell rang, kids rose from their desks quietly, and filed out.

In the hallway, Claire Richardson stood against the wall, holding her books against her skirt. Her long, dark hair was piled on top of her head. I acted like I didn't see her and started to go around, but she said to me, "Mark, is that true?"

"What?"

"That your dog went to Vietnam?"

"If he makes it through training . . ." I had practiced this scene in my head. How I would look off into the distance and not be able to speak. Claire would put her hand on my arm to comfort me.

It turned out I really couldn't say more—my throat shrank up so the words got stuck.

Claire looked at me hard. She didn't touch my arm, but she put her face close to mine, and I liked that.

"Why did you do that!"

I blinked. "What?"

"Didn't you like the dog? Were you trying to get rid of him?"

I stared at her. How could she think that? My throat was still shriveled up and I couldn't say anything.

"How could you? Vietnam!" Her chin came forward.

My mouth tried to make words. "I . . ."

Her face looked mad and not so pretty anymore.

I said, "I think he can help."

Her eyebrows pushed together. "Mark! Nothing can help over there."

I must have looked confused, because she said, "Where have you been? Asleep? Don't you read the papers? Or watch the news?" She moved toward the lockers, saying over her shoulder, "What an awful, awful thing to do to a dog."

* * *

I lifted the key from under the doormat and unlocked the back door. It felt weird to be using a key to get into my own house.

I stood on the welcome mat in the kitchen and braced myself. Then I remembered, Wolfie wouldn't be hurtling into the room like a rocket.

Mom used to say Wolfie should have been named Thunk. When I'd get home from school, he'd tear around the house from room to room, skidding on the floors, scattering the throw rugs, and running into furniture. Then he'd drink from the toilet, *glomp, glomp, slurp, glomp*, dribble water all over the bathroom floor, and want to lick me.

A note lay on the counter at the spot where Mom usually stood. Sometimes when I got home from school Mom would be vacuuming or folding clothes or clipping coupons at the table—but most times she was at the kitchen counter chopping vegetables or measuring ingredients for dinner.

I read the note.

Dear Mark,

Have milk with your cookies. Also, there is an apple with peanut butter in the fridge. Hope you had a good day at school.

At 5:30, would you put the casserole in the oven? It's on the bottom shelf of the fridge. Cook at 350° on the middle oven rack.

Love,
Mom

I crumpled up the note. If Mom had been home, I could have told her about what had happened in history class, but she had surprised us by announcing she was starting a job. I had thought I was going to have more time with her after Danny left. When Danny was still at home, he often took up the kitchen telling his show-off stories. And once or twice a week his band, the Invincible Tulip, would rehearse in the basement, making the whole house shake. I liked coming home to the racket, but Mom and I couldn't talk above it.

I listened to the kitchen wall clock go *click, click, click.* I peeked in the cookie jar. There were snickerdoodles, my favorite. Mom must have made them before she went to work.

I took my cookies and milk into the living room and sat down. The house felt empty.

Wolfie used to fill up a room, partly because he was as big as a piece of furniture, partly because of his attitude. A room with an excited dog in it hardly needs anything else.

Wolfie's big yellow sock toy lay on the bottom shelf of the bookcase. It had been his favorite, and he used to tear around the back yard with it in his mouth. One time I'd hidden the sock on the top rung of a ladder in the garage. Wolfie sniffed around, and when he realized where the sock was, scrambled up the rungs like he'd been climbing ladders all his life.

Wolfie had been a hilarious puppy who fell over his big feet and ran headlong into things if he was in a hurry. He was always in a hurry when he saw me. When I'd adopted him, a shelter volunteer had told me, "It's unusual for someone to pick the biggest of the litter. People often take the runt, because they feel sorry for it." I liked that Wolfie was largest, but that wasn't why I'd chosen him. I had picked up each of the four pups to compare them, and it was Wolfie who had burrowed into my neck, his fat belly against my bare skin.

Wolfie was my puppy, but the whole family had gotten involved in naming him. The woman at the animal shelter had said his mother was purebred German shepherd, so Danny wanted to give him a German name like Gus or Max. Dad said no, no German names. Dad had been in World War II. He didn't see any action or even get near any battles, but some men he was friends with in basic training got killed by the Germans.

"How about Adolf?" Danny had joked.

Dad gave Danny an awful look. "That is *not* funny."

Mom scowled, too.

Mom suggested Lad and Prince and Duke. Danny and I looked at her and said, "Geez, Mom," so she didn't suggest any others. I thought of Wolfgang, after Wolfgang Amadeus Mozart, because Dad loves Mozart more than anything. Dad teaches high school band and orchestra and is always raving about how Mozart was the smartest man who ever lived, smarter even than Einstein. Mozart records are playing a lot of the time at our house, and I could hum you all the pieces on *The Best of Mozart* by the New York Philharmonic.

Danny hissed at me, "No German names, Markmallow."

"Wolfgang would be okay; Wolfie for short," Dad said. "Mozart was Austrian."

Mom and Danny traded a look.

Danny followed Mom to the kitchen. I hurried after them.

"What?" I said.

"Mom! Hitler was Austrian," Danny said.

Mom put a finger to her lips. "Sh. Let's not look for consistency here." And then she gave in to a smile that showed her nice teeth.

Dad is inconsistent. He says we'll never buy a Volkswagen, but he loves sauerkraut, German sausage, Beethoven, German rye bread, and Mrs. Heimbach, our neighbor. Mrs. Heimbach may be different because she's a German Jew. The Germans treated Jews like they weren't even people, and that happened because Germany had a terrible government. In this country, laws don't let police bust into your house in the night or send you off to

27

prison camps or make people wear stars around their necks if they're a different religion. If it weren't for America, Dad says the Germans would have won WWII and they'd rule the world now and still be killing Jews and Gypsies and anyone else they decided to. America protects people in other countries, and that's what we're doing in Vietnam, making it safe for the Vietnamese.

* * *

A notebook lay on the coffee table. I reached for a pencil from the pencil can, and began to write.

"There once was a dog named Wolfie . . ."

I started through the alphabet looking for rhyming words. "Bolfie, Colfie, Cholfie . . ."

I gave up at *M*, scratched out what I'd written, and started over.

There once was a big happy pup
Who looked like he'd never grow up.
But he went to the service,
And that made him nervous,
So he turned back and came home . . .

I was searching for something that rhymed with *pup*. *To sup?* The phone saved me.

"Hi Mark." It was Dad. "I'm wrapping up band practice and will be heading home in a few minutes."

Dad rehearsed pep band three nights a week after school. Then he had a thirty-five-minute drive home.

"How's everything?"

"Okay," I said.

"Did your mom call?"

"No."

"I'm curious to know how everything is going. The first day on a job is tiring and she'll be wiped out tonight. Let's keep the house picked up, okay?"

"Okay."

* * *

When Dad arrived home he turned the TV on first thing. Dad didn't like TV news and thought people shouldn't have to watch the war in their homes. "We don't want to see our boys getting shot and carried away on stretchers," he said. "They shouldn't let journalists film that stuff." Before Danny left for Vietnam, Dad mostly read the paper for news.

But after Danny shipped out, Dad and I started watching TV news more. When soldiers were shown on the screen, we would sit closer, like we might get a glimpse of Danny.

The war news came on after a minute. It was pretty much the same night after night, soldiers in trucks or jeeps, shooting, explosions, and everyone running for cover.

This night, it showed a truck full of our soldiers arriving to help out guys who were pinned down in a firefight. The fresh troops hit the ground running and then dove for cover behind trees.

The newscaster said fifteen of our soldiers had been killed during the battle. Wounded soldiers were shown being carried to a helicopter on stretchers. There was a screaming Vietnamese woman running with a child in her arms.

Dad went to the kitchen to get a couple of cookies, then sat down in his recliner and opened the paper.

"Anything new with you?"

"Um, did Mom"—my voice came out funny, like I was talking into a glass—"start that job because of Danny?"

"What do you mean?"

"Because she's bored now that he's gone?"

"I don't think it's boredom. I think she's trying to get her mind off worrying about him. Also, she's got it in her head that we need money."

It surprised me that Mom had brought up money with Dad. She used to tell Danny and me that money was a delicate subject because Dad didn't make much as a teacher. "Don't pressure him for too many things," she'd say, "because he wants to be a good provider and hates to turn you down."

Dad fell asleep after he finished his cookies. I forgot to put the casserole in at 5:30, but it didn't matter because Mom, who'd said she'd be home at 6:00, didn't get home until 7:30.

She apologized about ten times, explaining that the library had gotten really busy and then, after the crowd thinned, a stack of books needed to be shelved so she had offered to do it.

"You could have called so we'd know you hadn't gotten in a car wreck." Dad lifted one eyebrow.

It wasn't exactly like Dad had been worried sick. He'd napped until ten minutes before Mom got home.

"We were so busy . . . " Mom said.

We ate supper without much conversation. Part of it was that Dad and I were so hungry we just shoveled in our food. Part of it was we were irritated at Mom that we were eating so late. I decided not to bring up my news from the day.

But after I went to bed and turned out the light, I

started turning Dorweiller's words over, wondering if they were true. If dogs were saving American soldiers, it made sense that the Vietcong would target them.

"Wolfie," I whispered into the dark. "You gotta flunk the training."

4

"How is your bruzzer?" Mrs. Heimbach called from her front sidewalk. Then she added with a grin, "Markmallow?"

When Effie Heimbach smiled, the side of her mouth pulled up, her head tilted, and her shoulders scrunched up. I never saw anyone who grinned with their whole body like that, unless I counted Wolfie.

"I dunno," I answered. She could have asked how *I* was. It so happened that my life was rotten, if anyone cared to find out. I hadn't been able to talk to Mom or Dad for a couple of days because they were so much busier now with Mom working. I missed Wolfie. And during American History I hadn't dared look at Claire Richardson, and that had always been the best part of class.

Then I felt guilty. Of course Mrs. Heimbach would ask about Danny. He was in danger, and me, I just went to junior high, which might seem like a war zone to me (three guys got kicked out of school last week for having knives hidden in their motorcycle boots) but isn't like

32

Vietnam, where people try to kill you with mortars and machine guns and hand grenades.

"We haven't heard from Danny for a couple of weeks," I told Mrs. Heimbach.

"Tsuh, tsuh, tsuh." Effie Heimbach wagged her finger. "He is a bad boy! He should write his muzzer because she is *vorried.*" But she said it with this huge, affectionate smile. Then, looking serious she said, "And how are you, Mark?"

I shrugged.

"What do you hear about Volfie?" Mrs. Heimbach brought her round face close.

Before I knew it I was telling her what Dorweiller had said about the Vietcong putting a bounty on the dogs in Vietnam.

"Ach, no!" Mrs. Heimbach slapped her hand against her cheek. "Not that nice *Volfie!*" She shook her silvery head. "Let us hope that is not the truth!" She chewed on a plump finger, her forehead all wrinkled up. Suddenly she looked at me. "Mark, I have rolls I baked today. You must come in, please."

I followed her to the house.

The warm-oven, cinnamon smell in Mrs. Heimbach's kitchen made me light-headed with hunger. She put down a purple placc mat for me, a white-and-purple plate, a linen napkin, and a fancy glass filled with milk.

"Don't go to a lot of trouble, " I said, not meaning it. I liked her fussing over me.

"So tell me now, who was the person who said this about Volfie?"

"Gene Dorweiller."

"A friend of yours?"

"No. Well, sort of. I talk to him when I'm waiting for

33

the bus, now that Rick has basketball practice."

"Oh, yes, Ricky, the one with freckles. But this Dor-weiller, he is a"—she searched for a word—"dependable boy?"

"No. He's a show-off always looking for attention."

"Ah!" Mrs. Heimbach brought a big knife down on the pan of rolls. "You see? This boy was trying to get noticed. Perhaps he make up the whole thing. To"—her head cocked; she looked like a smiling robin—"get your goats."

She set a roll in front of me. "Now, what else? How is everything at school? How is your muzzer's new job?"

Whether it was Mrs. Heimbach's sweet face or the way her house smelled, or that I didn't have anyone else to talk to, I started to pour out my troubles.

"I haven't seen Mom much the last couple days. School is . . . Something weird happened. With this girl."

Mrs. Heimbach wriggled. "A pretty girl? I'm thinking, yes?"

"Yeah. She's . . . cool. She's real smart. She doesn't sit there combing her hair all the time and putting on mascara. Sometimes she argues with Mr. Casey, not lipping off, but, like, debates with him."

"She thinks for herself." Mrs. Heimbach tapped her head with the big knife. It left flakes of pastry in her hair. "She has a good mind."

"Yeah."

"This is good, Mark, to like girls with clever minds. You want to marry such a girl so you will have smart children."

I was a long ways from having children, but I nodded anyway. My mind started to wander to the pages, "Reproductive Processes" that I'd looked up in the encyclopedia, but then I realized Mrs. Heimbach was waiting for me to go on.

I told her about Mr. Casey's remark in class, which she couldn't understand, either, and about Claire's saying that donating Wolfie to Vietnam had been a terrible thing to do.

Mrs. Heimbach's face, which was always moving, got immobile.

I said, "Claire asked me if I was asleep."

"Ahhh." Mrs. Heimbach nodded like she got the whole picture.

"What?"

"She is against the war. She thinks you don't know many people oppose it."

"Not many people, Mrs. Heimbach. Dad says a *few* people, hippies and fanatics, oppose the war, but most people in this country are patriotic."

"There is much turmoil in the country. What about the awful killings last year?"

"The assassinations didn't have anything to do with the war." The year before, Martin Luther King, Jr., got killed by someone who was against blacks getting equal rights, and then Bobby Kennedy, who was running for president, was killed by this nut guy named Sirhan Sirhan.

"This country has upheaval, Mark. Remember what happened at the Democratic convention in Chicago last summer?"

"Kind of. Hippies were carrying Vietcong flags and yelling dirty words at the police and throwing rocks and bottles."

"But the police! They beat the protesters, some of them children, some only because they carried a sign

35

against the war. They broke heads and arms and—" She stopped. She laid her hand on her chest and took a big breath. "Mark," she said, "you are a good boy to respect your parents."

Then she smiled and said, "Your roll is all gone! You must have anuzzer." So I did.

While I ate, Mrs. Heimbach showed me what she was embroidering for my mother for Christmas. We always have Mrs. Heimbach over for Christmas dinner. Mom lost her parents when she was in college, and Dad's parents live in Florida, so Mrs. Heimbach is a substitute parent and grandparent to us. Mrs. Heimbach's only relative in the U.S. is her nephew, Walter, a lawyer in Washington, D.C. Mom says he is brilliant, but one time when he was visiting I invited him to play Ping-Pong and he hardly knew how to hold the paddle. I had to show him everything.

It was time for me to go, and Mrs. Heimbach walked me to the door. She laid her hand on my shoulder and said, "Mark, I want you to call me Effie. In Germany, we were formal and called our elders not by their first names. But your bruzzer called me Effie, and I liked it."

"Okay. Effie." I thanked her again for the rolls, and walked back to my house, kind of wishing she hadn't brought up my "bruzzer," because for a while there, it had been just her and me.

* * *

The rest of the week went a lot like the first couple of days. Mom came home tired; Dad didn't talk much. I ducked out of American History every day to avoid Claire and disappeared into the pushing and shoving crowd. I stayed away from Dorweiller at the bus stop, and that meant I didn't have anyone to hang around with. As always, I made sure I didn't look at the guys who slunk around the bus stop spoiling for a fight.

Rick came over after basketball practice on Wednesday. We turned the radio on so loud the floor vibrated. I got out the encyclopedia and showed him the pages called "Reproductive Processes."

"I've seen these before," he said. The pictures were of men and women without clothes and without skin, their inside organs showing.

We went to Danny's room and looked under his mattress and in his closet for copies of *Playboy,* but couldn't find any. Rick was tired and didn't stay long.

It was the kind of week you would have liked to go to the park with your dog and throw balls for him and feel happy just doing something normal.

I was fidgety, like I'd stepped into someone else's life by mistake and nothing was the way it used to be. And then something happened that was so cool it nearly knocked me over.

I was coming out of history class, trying not to look around because I might see Claire Richardson, and there she was, blocking my path.

She gave me this real friendly look. You would never have known that the last time she'd spoken to me she'd kind of implied that I didn't know how to read.

"Mark," she said. For just a second, she looked bashful. She took a breath and said, "I wondered if you would go to the girls' choice dance with me?"

I stared at her. "Geez, yes," I said.

She smiled that great, no-braces smile of hers. "My dad will drive us. I asked him already. I'll write you a note about it, okay?"

"Sure." I couldn't hold back a grin of my own. Standing there smiling at each other, it didn't seem like we'd been almost enemies a few days before.

The girls' choice dance was ten days away. It wasn't even an after-school sock hop; it was from six to eight on a Friday night, and only for eighth graders. Claire was going to write me a note. Kids would see her hand it to me. And lots and lots of people would see me at the dance with her. Claire Richardson—tall, pretty Claire, who could have gotten anybody she wanted, any football or basketball player—had asked *me* to the girls' choice dance.

* * *

Friday night when I got home from school, I reached into the mailbox and found a letter addressed to me. The return address on it said, "Wolfie."

I didn't go in the house, even though it was a cold day, but sat down on the porch step and ripped the letter open.

September 22

Dear Mark,

Sarge give me your letter and told me to answer it. My name is Tucker Smalley, Pfc. Smalley now, from Spring Creek, Kentucky. I got assigned to Wolfie. No, that ain't right. He got assigned to me. HA!

Most dogs in our class was raised by the army, but three dogs come from private citizens. Wolfie is the only one of them who has got a letter, but Sgt. Garcia is making the other two handlers write letters to their dogs' former owners, too. You started something.

38

I reread that paragraph. I didn't like the sound of "former owners." Wolfie was on loan to the army.

Me and Wolfie are in our third week together. The first two weeks, the dogs were in quarantine, but we started working on basic obedience anyway. They start-ed us with ten-minute lessons, followed by ten-minute breaks. That was a good thing for ole Wolfie because he could hardly pay attention that long. I used to think I wasn't much for school, but Wolfie makes me look pret-ty good.

I started to feel sad. Wolfie was such a wonderful dog, I had been sure his handler would feel lucky to have him.

Then we worked up to 15 minutes, followed by 15-minute breaks; now we are at 20 minutes. You asked how much of the day dogs are in training. The soldiers have a lot of appointments—getting shots to go overseas and orientation classes and meetings with the finance officer. But on a day when I don't have no appoint-ments, I work with Wolfie 6 to 8 hours.
Peterson is looking over my shoulder and correcting my spelling. At this rate, it's going to take forever to answer your questions.

The letter was messy with scratch-outs. The guy wasn't too smart; no wonder he didn't understand what a great dog Wolfie was.

I transferred to this program because they was ask-ing for volunteers. Being infantry, I knew I'd be going on patrols in the jungle looking for Charlie. I figured I'd be better off with a dog than without one. I been around dogs all my life. I have two hounds at home I hunt with. They pay a lot better attention than Wolfie.

Me and Wolfie got paired up because Sgt. Garcia says it's good to put a under aggressive dog like Wolfie with a aggressive handler. Wolfie is the most under aggressive dog in the class of twelve. Lucky me, huh? I guess that makes me the most aggressive handler. Not to brag, but I do win most any fight I get into.

My hands had started to shake from the cold, and the cement step I was sitting on felt like an ice block. I went in the house, put the teapot on the stove, and opened a package of hot chocolate.

While I was waiting for the water to warm, I started to see the letter differently. Sure, it was hard to think about Wolfie spending his days with someone who didn't like him much. But I had been hoping Wolfie wouldn't make it through training. This Smalley guy made it sound like Wolfie didn't have what it took.

When Wolfie got home, I'd never again get mad at him when he came blasting into the room and knocked me off balance.

I sat down in the living room with my hot chocolate and picked up the letter.

You asked how we disiplin the dogs. When we are training, we use choke collars on them. If they don't pay attention to a command, we give them a jerk. It don't hurt them. When we are doing exercises in the field, like chasing decoy soldiers, the dogs wear harnesses. That way they know they are on a mission.

40

*Sgt. Garcia said he'd personally whup anybody
who mistreated a dog. Not that I would. Dogs, in my
personal opinion, are better than most humans. I
always took up for my dogs if somebody in my family
wanted to be hard on them, which happened when they
was drunk. The people, not the dogs. HA!*

*Pardon all the scratching out. English was my
worst subjeck, but I didn't exactly set no records in any
of them.*

*I hope I answered your questions. It was nice of you
to donate your dog. He may not be a natural like some,
but he'll do. Sgt. Garcia said there is a chance Wolfie
and me will have to go back and repeat the first couple
weeks of training. They keep working a dog until the
dog gets it.*

I froze. I almost couldn't go back and reread the last
couple sentences. Did that mean what it sounded like?
That if Wolfie didn't do well, they'd just keep recycling
him in training? *They keep working a dog until the dog
gets it.*

The letter was signed, "Sincerely, Pfc. Tucker
Smalley."

I took a sip of hot chocolate and spilled it onto my
shirt and the coffee table. Some splashed onto the other
mail I'd brought in. I dabbed at the letters with the tail of
my shirt, and noticed that one was from Danny. I grabbed
it up. It smelled like a bath towel that has been on the bedroom floor a week.

It was addressed to us all, but I ripped it open. A piece
of folded notebook paper fell out, separate from the other
pages. On it was written *Marco Polo*.

I laughed when I opened it because it was about three

sentences long. Leave it to Danny to write as short a letter as he could.

On the top it said, "August 8." Danny's first letter had taken only a week or so to get to us. Something must have slowed this one down.

> *Marconi,*
>
> *If you can, stop the plan to donate Wolfie. I've had my eyes opened on a few things, and see it's not a good idea.*
>
> *Hope this gets to you in time.*
> *Your everlovin' brother,*
> *Danny*

5

I stared at the letter. Danny had written it before he got my letter telling him about delivering Wolfie to the army post.

I walked to the kitchen, hoping Mom had miraculously appeared at the counter. Why wasn't she around? She used to be for Danny. Did we need money all that bad?

I went back and sat down on the sofa again. Soldiers were in Vietnam for a year; that's what Danny said. He'd been there since June; now it was September. Eight more months to go. Maybe dogs had the same duty time. A year wasn't so awful long.

I took the thumbtack out of the calendar on the kitchen wall and started paging through it. Training was twelve weeks, longer if Wolfie had to repeat some of it. Then he and his handler would go to Vietnam. December would be the earliest Wolfie would arrive there.

Our calendar ended with December 1969. I flung it down on the counter. If I could see December 1970, its days lined up and numbered in an orderly way, I would feel better.

I went to my room and got money out of my top drawer, got on my bike, and pedaled down to Lindstrom's Drug. I told the clerk I needed to buy a 1970 calendar.

She was a gray-haired woman who wore her hair off her face, and her name tag said *Marlene*. She said they didn't have new calendars yet, but would by the end of the month.

I rode home real slow. I sat on the porch shivering instead of going into the empty house.

* * *

Dad had his first band concert of the year that night, so he had decided to stay at school. I heated the casserole Mom had left for me and sat down in front of the TV. Wolfie's yellow sock toy glared at me from the bookcase. I set down my plate, went over and picked up the toy, and put it in the closet out of sight.

The front doorbell rang. I lifted the drape and looked out. Effie Heimbach stood on the porch with a tray in her hands. Her nose and cheeks were red from the cold and she was blinking snowflakes off her lashes.

"Come in, Effie. When did it start snowing?"

"Only a few minutes ago." She looked around. "Where are your parents?"

"Not home right now."

"You are eating supper. Go on, you must finish."

"I can wait."

"Sit down!" she ordered. I did.

"I come over to show you something I make." Her mouth pulled up in that ultimate grin of hers.

"Rolls?" I started to grin, too.

44

"No, not this time." Her smile started to collapse.

"Something for Danny," I said.

Effie looked sheepish. "Soon, I make rolls for you and something nice to send Danny. Today, I make treats for someone else." Her elfish expression returned. "You would like to see?"

"Sure."

Effie, watching my face, lifted the towel on the tray.

"Wow," I said.

"You like?"

Big dog biscuits, shaped like bones, lined up in neat rows on the tray. "Those are so cool. You made them yourself?"

"The newspaper had a recipe for dog treats. It said to cut them into strips. It was my idea to make them into bones."

"How did you do it?"

She bent over the tray. "I take dough, I curl up ends, like so? Then I press"—she shoved the heel of her hand down—"and they look like bones, yes?"

"They look good enough to eat. Can I have one?"

"Ach, you silly thing, you would spit out and waste, and all my work for nothing."

"When are you going to send them?"

"Tomorrow."

I got out Tucker's letter and wrote the address for her. "I bet Wolfie will be the only dog who gets packages with homemade dog biscuits."

Effie beamed. Then her face got instantly sad. "I miss him. Always, when I am outside and you and Volfie are coming down the street, and he look up"—she imitated a dog lifting its muzzle—"and see me and yah! he is happy. When I met him he was puppy, and I thought, 'This dog will be too big for Mark.' But when he grows up to be oh so loving, I see God must give him big body to make room for such a heart."

I nodded.

"I have made you sad." Effie touched my arm.

"These are great, Effie."

"Mark, dogs have the good noses, yes?"

"Yeah."

"Volfie will know the biscuits come from me? His nose, it will tell him?"

"Wolfie's got an unbelievable nose. He'll know they're from you."

Effie's plump cheeks flushed. "That's nice." She laid the towel carefully over the tray, and went back into the snowy night.

* * *

I huddled over my school desk and wrote:

An army dog handler named Smalley
Put his head down and started to bawl-y.
"I wanted a mean dog,
A combat-machine dog,
But this one is happy and jolly."

Mr. Casey tapped my arm, motioned for me to show him the sheet of paper I was writing on. Slowly I moved my arm and revealed the limerick.

"Doesn't look like history notes, Mark."

I stared at my fingers, which had a death grip on my pencil.

"I'll take this." He slipped the paper off my desk. "I'd

46

like you to come see me after school today." He said it so quietly that only Dorweiller, in front of me, and Teresa, the fat girl behind me, heard.

After Mr. Casey walked off, Dorweiller turned around with pig eyes wide and his mouth twisted, about to make some stupid comment. I gave him the meanest, coldest look I could, and, surprisingly, he turned around and faced the front of the room.

* * *

Mr. Casey was bent over his desk when I got to his room after school. A couple of fluorescent lights overhead were burned out, so the room was dim. I stood in the doorway a minute, then walked across the room and sat down in a front desk. Still, Mr. Casey didn't look up.

He had pinned pictures above the blackboards. Washington on a white horse. Lincoln standing next to a desk. Next to Lincoln hung a giant Gettysburg Address. Mr. Casey had put a red circle around the words *government of the people, by the people, for the people.*

I thought he was correcting papers, but then I saw he had a small book in his palms. *Sonnets.* He looked up, like I'd caught him smoking in the boys' bathroom. "Mark!" He shut the book and slapped it onto his desk. "I didn't hear you come in."

He laid his hands on top of his desk and gave me a pleasant look. Strands of black curly hair had strayed onto his forehead.

I waited.

Mr. Casey was in his second year of teaching. He'd learn to be a little stricter, I thought. But a lot of kids, especially the girls, thought he was their best teacher.

"So, Mark," he said after a minute. "What's on your—" He stopped suddenly, like he'd just returned to his body from outer space. "Oh, yeah. I asked you to . . ."

He stood up, came over, and pulled up a student desk from the next row. When he lowered himself into it, his legs stuck out like a spider's.

"Mark, I'm noticing some things I'd like to talk to you about."

"Okay."

"The last exam I gave, for one thing. You didn't do too well."

I looked up. "No?" I tried to remember the test—whether it was hard and what the questions were. I couldn't recall anything about it, though I had a faint memory of taking it.

"I think you were guessing on the multiple choice. In the past, you have expressed yourself well on essay questions, but this time you gave one-line answers that didn't convince me you knew the material. Were you feeling all right when you took the test?"

"I think so."

"Your class participation has changed, too."

I looked at him. I'd hardly ever participated.

"You've always been fairly quiet," Mr. Casey said, "but when you do offer something, it's right on target. Others in the class look forward to hearing what you think about a subject, sort of wait to hear your ideas to make up their minds."

I blinked. "My ideas?"

"Yeah. When I ask for opinions about something, your classmates look your way. I think they miss hearing from you."

That couldn't be right. If kids looked my way, I'd notice it. Kids in Mr. Casey's class, particularly girls, waited for Dorweiller to do his show-off thing, not for me to say something.

"You don't believe me. Okay. Let's go on. I wondered about this limerick you wrote."

He stretched over and rustled papers on his desk, then came up with the one he'd taken from me. He read the limerick in silence, then handed it to me.

I had forgotten what it said. When I read it, a pain started in my throat. I felt like I did one time when I was about six, at a birthday party. The cake or the mints or something didn't agree with me and I felt like throwing up, but of course you can't do that at a birthday party, so I stood in a corner by myself and made my chest and stomach as tight as I could so sour frosting couldn't wash up the pipes in my throat.

That's how I felt sitting in that desk in Mr. Casey's dim room. Not like I'd puke, but like I might do something worse. My lips had started to tremble.

"Who is Smalley?"

"Tucker Smalley." It wasn't a subject I wanted to talk about. "He's a soldier at Fort Benning."

"The one who works with your dog?"

"Yeah." He remembered what Dorweiller had blabbed in class? "Only, I'm not sure Wolfie's my dog anymore. The army may think he belongs to them."

"What kind of agreement do you have with them?"

I shrugged. "My dad talked to them. I thought I was loaning Wolfie."

"But you're not sure?"

I shook my head. "Dad told me the World War II dogs came home to their owners after the war was over. Or sometimes, owners gave permission for soldiers to take dogs home with them because they'd been through so much together."

The furnace kicked off, and the room went still.

After a minute Mr. Casey said, "This dog handler is . . . what? Frustrated with Wolfie?"

I nodded.

Mr. Casey waited for me to say more. I studied the side of my tennis shoe, which was developing a rip.

"I suppose you think Wolfie is okay the way he is."

"He's a lot better than okay! He's crazy happy all the time. Even though he's huge and has giant teeth that show because he's always smiling, little kids, even ones in strollers, want to reach out and touch him. They can tell he's a teddy bear."

Mr. Casey smiled. "He sounds like a dog anyone would go for."

"He wants to please, too. Because he's so big and excited, he sometimes knocks things over and makes a mess, but when you scold him, he flops down on the floor, stretches out, and covers his eyes with a paw."

"It's good to see you smile, Mark."

I got self-conscious then, and shut up.

"So, this dog handler didn't click with him, but some other handler might have been really pleased with him."

"He's not aggressive enough for this guy. It sounds like Wolfie might not be aggressive enough for what the army wants."

"Maybe you can get him back."

"I was hoping he'd flunk out. But they don't flunk them out—they just send them through training again."

Mr. Casey looked at me a long time before saying, "May I ask you something?"

"Yeah."

"Why did you send him?"

I think he meant, why did I send a dog that wasn't suited for army work?

"They were looking for German shepherds." I pulled a thread from the button on my sleeve and wound it around my thumb. "And he's smart and loyal. I thought he might save soldiers' lives."

"You thought he might save boys like your brother."

The way he said it, I felt proud. "Yeah. How did you know my brother was over there?"

"I know which students have relatives—dads or brothers—over there. There are seventeen in the school." Mr. Casey glanced at the clock. "Do you have a bus to catch?"

"Yeah. Five minutes."

"You'd better get going. But I'd like to hear more about Wolfie and how he's doing. Stop by after school sometime, okay?"

"Do you like dogs or something?"

"I like dogs a lot. I have two."

"What kind?"

"Mutts."

"Cool." I pulled on my jacket. "Can I ask you something?"

"Sure."

"Why don't we talk about Vietnam in here?"

Mr. Casey twisted in the small desk. He tightened his hand on the edge of it and looked at me. I think he was weighing whether to answer.

"I've been ordered by the school board not to."

"Oh." I wanted to know more about that, but I had to catch my bus.

I was just about to the door when Mr. Casey said, "Mark, remember something about our system. We are in charge. The citizens. The military, government employees, members of Congress, even the president—they work for us."

6

On Saturday, I got up late. Mom met me in the kitchen, grinning. She had gotten her first paycheck from the library, and she proudly handed me five dollars.

"You and Rick go to the A&W and get yourselves hamburgers and floats."

"Thanks." I gazed at the five-dollar bill. I wasn't in the mood for a hamburger, but I could spend the five dollars on something for Wolfie. Or something for Private Smalley. If I was nice to him, maybe he'd be good to Wolfie. "I'll save it," I said.

"No sir," Mom said. "You've been cooped up here by yourself too much. You spend that money on something fun. Besides, you hardly ever get to see Rick anymore."

She looked so pleased, like she'd granted me my biggest wish, so I didn't have the heart to tell her that what I really wanted to do was sit in the kitchen while she cut up a chicken and talk to her about Danny's letter to me and the one from Tucker Smalley.

I had shown Tucker's to her the day it arrived. In the

places where Smalley talked about Wolfie being a disappointment, Mom had said, "Oh," in a sad way. I'll give her this, she didn't say a word about having told Dad and me that Wolfie would have trouble paying attention. But we didn't have much time to talk then, and we hadn't since.

Rick jumped at the chance for a trip to the A&W. He arrived at my house ten minutes after I called him.

It was a sunny day, but nippy. We rode our bikes, and when we got there we were too cold to order floats, so we got hot chocolate with extra whipped cream and fries and hamburgers. After we ate, we went to Rick's house.

I lay on his little brother's bed, staring at the ceiling. The light fixture had a design of small ovals with dots in the center, like eyeballs.

The great thing about Rick was—well, everything was great about Rick. If you wanted to talk, he'd listen. If you wanted to say nothing, he was happy to leave you alone. A lot of times I'd forget to ask him how he was doing, but he never forgot to ask me how things were going.

Rick lay on the other twin bed, which had a brown bedspread that matched the cowboys on the wallpaper. I guess the wallpaper was left over from when Rick was younger, or else it was for his little brother, Greg, who shared the room.

Finally I said, "How's basketball?"

"Good. Goes good."

With Rick, that might mean anything. The year before, he had been the only seventh grader to move up to junior varsity. He didn't bother mentioning it, and I'd heard the news at school. Turned out he had shot so many baskets that the junior varsity coach just about turned inside out watching him.

"Does 'goes good' mean you might be playing for the high school team?"

Rick smiled. "No, doesn't mean that." He leaned up on his elbow and called out the doorway. "Go on, Greg, we got forty minutes left."

Greg, who looked a lot different from Rick, had a mop of dark curly hair and no freckles. He scowled around the doorway at me. "Don't play with my stuff," he warned.

"I won't," I promised.

"Go on!" Rick had bribed Greg with a quarter to leave us alone for an hour.

It got quiet in the room again, both of us gazing at the ceiling.

I asked, "Do you think a guy is awful if he misses his dog more than his own brother?"

"I'd miss my dog more than Greg."

"You don't have a dog."

"I'd miss the dog I don't have more than I'd miss Greg."

"You've got reasons to get annoyed with Greg. He's a little kid who's always trailing you around. But Danny is a pretty good older brother."

Rick nodded. "I like him." Then he added, "Not as much as I like you."

Of course he'd like me better. Still, I didn't mind hearing him say it.

"Danny is miserable, and I don't want him miserable," I said. "And I don't want him to get hurt. But it's Wolfie who is on my mind all the time."

Rick flipped over onto his stomach. "Cantrell, you are o-kay. And don't think you're not."

55

"If Danny got hurt . . ."

"It wouldn't be your fault," Rick said.

I was quiet.

"It wouldn't be your fault because you worried more about Wolfie."

"You sure?"

"Positive."

I took a deep breath. "Want to go to my house and play tetherball?"

Rick jumped up. "When Greg asks if he can come, the answer is no."

* * *

Mom had to work Saturday afternoon, helping with an inventory. After Rick went home, I raided the kitchen for snacks. Mom had left cheese-filled celery sticks in the refrigerator and muffins in the cookie jar. We would eat late that night because Mom wouldn't be home until 7:00. Under the old rules, I wasn't supposed to ruin my dinner, but under a new policy, Dad and I had big snacks so we didn't get ravenous and cross.

I lay down on the sofa with Danny's letters, the one to me, and the one to Mom and Dad. I'd reread mine a dozen times, feeling sick on the words, *Stop the plan to donate Wolfie.* I had read his note to Mom and Dad only once, so I unfolded it.

Dear Mom and Dad,

I was going to make a joke about mold growing on me, but I went on patrol with a guy yesterday who really does have a mold infection on his toes. It's ugly!

I'll spare you a description of the insects and their size, Mom. You would freak out.

*A few days ago, we took a hill. Then, for some
unknown reason, the lieutenant called us back. One
soldier lost his life taking that hill and another got
injured. I guess we'll have to take it again tomorrow.
It's hard to figure out what the point is.*

*I saw Tom Martin—remember him?—that I used
to run around with in elementary school. He's been here
six months. He says you get so nothing surprises you
anymore.*

*We are soaked and dirty and short on supplies. We
hear about guns jamming when you need them the
most, and I've had it happen myself during practice.*

*Would you send me Shelley Adams's address? I
think I'll write her.*

Love,

Danny

* * *

I fell asleep on the sofa with the TV on and a half-
eaten celery stick clutched in my hand. I woke up to find
Dad standing over me, eyebrows all knotted up.

"You okay?" he asked.

"Sure."

"We're out of milk. Want to walk down to the store
with me?"

"Okay." I pulled myself up, took a noisy bite of the
warm celery stick, and felt around under the coffee table
for my shoes.

We had gone only about a half block when Dad said,
"Want to go back for your gloves?"

I shook my head. I drove my hands into my jeans
pockets.

"At least put up your hood."

I shook my head again, even though my ears had started to sting.

"Seems cold for this time of year, doesn't it? I hope this doesn't mean that we're going to have a hard winter," Dad said.

I ducked my head against the wind.

"How's everything going, Mark?"

"Okay." What could I say? Admit that, except for going to the girls' choice dance with Claire at the end of next week, everything stunk?

"You've been quiet lately."

"I've always been quiet." I almost added, "I'm the son who *isn't* the life of the party, remember?" but Dad would think that was lippy, and it sounded whiny even to me.

"We've had so many changes in our family, with Danny leaving, Eve going to work, Wolfie leaving. Your mom and I are concerned about you, Mark."

I glanced over at him, and for the first time noticed how much scalp showed on the top of his head. We'd all teased him pretty bad when he started losing his hair, but he had gotten a lot more bald since—when? Since the last time I'd really looked at him.

"Dad," I said. "Put your hood up. You'll get cold."

He smiled. "I'll put mine on if you put yours on."

We stopped, pulled up our hoods, and tied them under our chins.

As we stood there, a young woman glided past us wearing what looked like a tarp. She said in a Twilight Zone voice, "May peace be yours this day."

I turned. "Hi, Agate."

"Who is *that*?"

"She lives here." I pointed.

Dad looked at the house and yard. "It gets worse all

58

the time. Those mattresses weren't in the yard before."

The lawn was littered with junk that spilled out onto the sidewalk near our feet. We couldn't see this house from ours, but Mom's friend lived across the street and said that fifteen to twenty people seemed to be living there, coming and going at odd hours.

"How do you know her name?"

"I met her when I used to walk Wolfie. She has a baby named Orion who liked to pet Wolfie."

"She's Agate and the baby is Orion? Those can't be their real names."

I shrugged.

Dad looked over the yard again. He sighed, "These are the people who think they can run the country better."

* * *

Sevorn's A&P, where Danny used to work, had chipped outside paint and scuffed floors. Rick and I always went on our bikes to the new Safeway, but Mom and Dad were loyal to Mr. Sevorn because Danny had worked for him.

"Randall!" Mr. Sevorn called. "How are you? What can I get you?"

"We need milk and maybe a few oranges."

"I just got some beautiful new oranges in," Mr. Sevorn said.

I looked away and grinned. Danny used to do a great imitation of Mr. Sevorn that would make Mom laugh so hard she'd clasp her hands across her mouth and almost choke. No matter what customers were looking for, Mr. Sevorn always had just gotten a *bee-u-tiful* new shipment of it. Danny would wet his hair, slick it back on the sides like Mr. Sevorn, and make his face real smiley.

"Potatoes? Oh, you bet! We just got a bee-u-tiful batch in. Brown the color of nuts, hardly any eyes in them. Walnuts? Oh, sure, just got some bee-u-tiful ones, superior quality. Brown the color of potatoes."

Dad leaned over the orange bin, selecting oranges.

"How is Danny doing?" Mr. Sevorn asked.

Dad, not a grinny person, got as grinny as Mr. Sevorn. "Oh, he's doing good."

My head snapped around.

Dad glanced at me. "Oh, there are rain and bugs and snakes. Snakes twelve feet long, and poisonous. But Danny's glad to be there for his country."

I stared at Dad. Danny didn't sound glad at all.

"Well, we know about that don't we, Randall?" Mr. Sevorn said. "You go where your country sends you, even if it's a miserable hellhole."

Dad nodded.

"And they're always hellholes, right? The army doesn't send you to resorts."

Dad nodded his head firmly. "Danny's unit took a hill from Charlie and they're holding it. Charlie's getting some tough lessons from our boys." His smile widened.

That's not what Danny had said.

I couldn't quit staring at Dad, suspended above the orange bin, smiling and nodding. I got a feeling there was something, like the advancing baldness, that I had been overlooking, but even though I studied him until my eyes hurt, I couldn't see what it was.

* * *

I cornered Mom on Sunday afternoon when she was folding clothes in the bedroom.

"Of *course* I have time," she said when I told her I had something on my mind.

"Do you think we could call the army today? Fort Benning?"

Her eyebrows lifted.

"I want to find out how we can get Wolfie back. It doesn't sound like they like him much, and he needs to be here, where people appreciate him. After Danny's letter, I don't want him to go to Vietnam."

Mom nodded. "I don't think we knew what a hole there would be in our lives with him gone." She searched for a mate to a green sock in the pile of clothes spread out on the bed. "But by now, they've invested time and money in training him and he is bonded with his handler."

"That dummy?"

"Mark." She frowned at me. "It's not his fault school didn't come easy for him. He might be smart in other ways."

"Like, he might have good judgment about dogs?"

She looked up from folding an undershirt and grinned. "Okay, he's a dope. But we don't know if the army lets dogs come home once they've been in training. Seems to me it would set a bad precedent."

"Most of the dogs in training are military dogs. Maybe they keep them in the program even if they're not doing well because there's no place else to send them. But it's different with Wolfie. He can come back to us."

"It won't hurt to ask, I guess. We'll get the phone number from information. Tomorrow probably is a better time to call. Maybe your dad—" And then she stopped. We looked at each other, and both knew what the other was thinking.

"Can we leave Dad out of this?" I asked.

Mom folded a washcloth—in half, in quarters, in eighths. She laid it by itself gently, like it was made of china. I knew what she was going to say. That Dad needed to be included in the discussion. That Dad should make the phone call because he knew his way around the army and because he had made the original contact. That Dad might have a view on the matter we ought to consider.

"Yes," she said. Just like that. "Would you like to talk to them yourself?"

"I would."

"Remember, there's a two-hour time difference.

"Yeah." I glanced over my shoulder. "Where is Dad?"

"He's on the sofa asleep."

Mom and I didn't look at each other after that. She kept her eyes down, searching for sock mates.

7

The poster showed two red stick figures dancing underneath a yellow moon outlined in black. Below the figures, someone had lettered the words,

Don't Miss the
Girls' Choice Harvest Dance!!
8th Graders Only.
Girls, Ask Your Favorite Guy!
6–8 P.M. Friday.

I stood in the hallway beside the cafeteria and gazed at the poster. It was Monday, and still no word from Claire.

Rick came up just then, pretended to trip, and fell into me. "Whatcha readin'?" He looked at the poster, then pointed at the figures. He said in a girlish voice, "You and Claire, dancing in the moonlight."

"If she hasn't forgotten and asked somebody else."

"No way. She needs to go with someone who matches her in intelligence. She hasn't said anything to me, so she must still be taking you."

"So people are pairing up according to brains?" I busted up laughing, because Cindy Cook, who was taking Rick, was dumber than mud.

Rick smiled in his easygoing way. "I won't be embarrassed to be with Cindy."

"No kidding." Cindy had boobs like the high school girls who hung around Danny.

"Anyway, you don't go to a dance to talk trigonometry. Hey, you don't really think Claire forgot?"

I blew air out my cheeks. "The way things are going . . ."

Just then Claire came into view, walking toward me in her graceful way that looked like floating. "There you are," she said, and handed me a note.

Rick melted away to leave me alone with her, but Claire didn't stay, just smiled and glided on.

I didn't rip the note open right there because it wouldn't have been cool. I didn't open it in my next class, either, because I didn't want to risk it being confiscated.

So I sat in English, the note burning in my pocket, trying to predict what it would say.

Mark. Let's cancel on the dance. Girls sometimes changed their minds.

Then I fell into dreaming the other way. The note would be mushy like the ones girls used to send in third grade. *Mark. I love you very much. I think about you all the time.*

I read the note in the boys' bathroom after English, and was relieved and disappointed both.

Mark,
  My dad will pick you up at 5:30. Please write me a

64

note with your address and directions on how to get to
your house.
    I think it will be fun, and I'm glad you can go.
        Claire

I read the last sentence over and over. *I think it will be fun, and I'm glad you can go.* That meant she liked me, right? I couldn't find anything negative in those words, though not getting my hopes up seemed a smarter policy than it used to.

* * *

"Hi. This is Mark Cantrell," I rehearsed before picking up the phone to dial the Fort Benning number Mom had left me. My voice had deepened and hardly ever jumped up anymore. Maybe I'd sound older than I was.

When I heard buzzes and knew the phone was ringing on the other end, my fingers began to drum the counter. Maybe I should have written a script.

"Captain Lenz speaking."

I stared at the phone. Already? I thought I would get his secretary or someone.

"Hi." It came out high and weak. From Dad, who'd taught hundreds of kids how to play horns, I knew that breath was everything, in speaking as well as in playing instruments. I took a huge breath and blew it out.

"My name is Mark Cantrell." Much better. "I sent my dog, Wolfie, to you, and he is in training as a scout dog."

"Uh-huh." Our names didn't seem to mean anything to him. "What may I help you with? Mike, was it?"

"Mark. I have some questions about donating a dog. If the dog doesn't show much promise"—I was proud of that; it sounded like something Dad would say—"does the army return it to its owners?"

"When you donated your dog, Mark, it became property of the U.S. Army. If a dog is unsuitable for one kind of program, it's transferred to a program where the dog might work out better. For instance, we train scout dogs here. When dogs are too aggressive for that kind of work, we transfer them to another facility to be trained as sentry dogs."

"What happens to dogs who aren't aggressive enough?"

"I don't think I've heard of any that weren't. Usually, German shepherds just take to scout dog training; they have it in their blood."

I didn't know what to say.

"What gives you the impression the dog you donated isn't working out?"

Inhale. I didn't want to get Tucker in trouble because I wanted to get more letters from him, and also I didn't want him taking anything out on Wolfie.

"Nothing," I said. "It's just that we're missing him more than we thought we would, and I hoped if he wasn't working out . . ."

"That you could have him back?" Captain Lenz gave a scornful chuckle. "No, it doesn't work like that. By now, the army has an investment in him. When did you send him?"

"End of August."

"The army paid to have Wilford shipped here—"

"Wolfie," I corrected.

"—and the dog has had a thorough exam by a veterinarian, inoculations, and a handler assigned to him. The dog and the handler begin to bond from the first days and it would be unfair to take a dog away from his handler only because the dog is missed at home." The captain cleared his throat. "Wolfie will be rendering a service for our country. Try to imagine what it's like for the families of soldiers, Mark. They feel like you do, missing their sons or brothers or fathers. But we can't send soldiers home because their families miss them."

"My brother is in Vietnam," I said, annoyed.

He went on like he hadn't heard. "When a private citizen donates a dog, he is breaking ties with the animal. Wolfie isn't a pet anymore; he's a soldier." The captain made his voice ring on those last words.

I stared at the phone. There was nothing more to say. I wished then that I hadn't let myself dream about getting Wolfie back.

"I hope this has been helpful, Mark. Here's something you might think about."

I waited.

"You could get yourself another dog."

If Mom hadn't drilled manners into me, I would have hung up on him. Instead, I said, "Thanks."

* * *

Mom put dinner on the table as soon as she got home, and the three of us sat down to eat. Mom gave me an inquisitive look and I shook my head. We glanced sideways at Dad in a guilty way.

"I'll help you with the dishes," I said in a too-loud voice when Mom started to clear the table.

"That's nice of you, Mark," Dad mumbled. His eyes hung at half-mast. He had tough Mondays. He taught band on Mondays, Wednesdays, and Fridays, and a lot of kids took band as a goof-off class. Dad loved music so much, he couldn't bear to hear it murdered. On Tuesdays and Thursdays he taught orchestra, which was better, because kids who signed up for that class were more serious about playing.

"What did they say?" Mom asked as soon as Dad had shuffled off to the living room.

"No deal. Wolfie is army property now. The captain said the army has already invested time and money in him."

"I was afraid of that." She gave me a worried look. "What happens later?"

"What do you mean?"

"I'm wondering about the statement that Wolfie is army property. After the war ends, then what? How about after he's served in Vietnam?"

"I assume I'll get him back. They wouldn't need him anymore."

"Did you ask how long dogs stay in Vietnam?"

"I forgot. I felt kind of shook up after he said there was no chance of getting Wolfie out of the training program."

"Would you want to call him back and ask him those questions?"

"No, but I might see if Tucker could find out." I pulled a spiral notebook from the kitchen drawer.

Dear Tucker,
   I was sorry to hear that Wolfie isn't doing too well in training.

I didn't mention my conversation with the captain. I asked Tucker if he could find out how long dogs stayed in Vietnam and what would happen to the dogs after the war. I also asked him if it was true that the North

Vietnamese had put a bounty on military dogs.

I meant to make it short, but I got started talking about Wolfie, and before I knew it, I'd done another six-pager. I included the story of Wolfie's first birthday.

When Wolfie turned a year old, my buddy Rick and I planned a party for him. I wanted Mom to make a chocolate cake, but she had read somewhere that dogs couldn't have chocolate, so we had angel food. We invited the Thompsons' cat, who comes over to our yard a lot. Wolfie wouldn't wear his party hat, but the cat liked hers and posed while Danny took her picture. After that, she wasn't a very good guest. She pounced on a sparrow in the patio and killed it. She carried it around in front of Wolfie, brushing against him and teasing him. If Wolfie so much as put his nose near the bird, the cat would swell up and moan and Wolfie would shrink back and look disappointed. Rick and I gave Wolfie a plate of cake and ice cream to make him feel better and he bolted it in two bites and then ate the paper plate.

In case you're interested, Wolfie's birthday is November 27. He will turn three.

I went on to tell Tucker about the tricks I'd taught Wolfie, like jumping through a hoop, that he'd learned in only a few lessons. "Wolfie may be under aggressive," I told him, "but he's really smart."

On Wednesday during American History, when I looked over at Claire she was gazing at me and talking to the girl who sits behind her. She waved three fingers and smiled. I lifted my hand in a wave, and then, not knowing what to do next, looked down at my desk.

Friday afternoon, I didn't get home until 4:30. Mom had ordered a corsage for Claire from Hill's Florist and I had to go there on my bike to pick it up. It was a white orchid with pink rosebuds and pink ribbon.

I jumped in the shower and then put on my good shirt and dress pants. I warmed the pan of stew Mom had left for me, and had eaten about half of it when the doorbell rang.

It was Claire.

8

Claire Richardson's dad leaned across the front seat of his Impala and reached for my hand.

"Mark. I'm Nathan Richardson."

I reached in and shook his hand. "I'm Mark." Then I realized he knew that; he'd called me by name.

Claire opened the car's back door. She was trying not to look at me. I managed not to look at her either, except for noticing that her hair was down and curling all over her shoulders.

Mom had told me to open Claire's doors for her, but I was too late. She had crawled into the backseat. The back door was still open.

I climbed into the front seat and closed my door. I tried to smile at Mr. Richardson, who didn't make a move to start the car. He glanced over his shoulder at Claire. Then it dawned on me; I had screwed up. I should have sat in the back with Claire because we were on a date, only I was sitting in the front seat with her dad.

I thought I should get out and get in the back with

Claire, but my arms and legs had frozen. So instead I said to her dad, kind of casual and man-to-man, "What kind of gas mileage you get with this Impala?"

Claire pulled the back door shut. "Just go, Nathan," she said.

"I get twenty on the road, about sixteen in town." He started the engine.

It was only a mile and a half to the junior high, but it turned out to be a long trip. I thought I could make things better if I turned around and talked to Claire, but my neck wouldn't swivel.

Facing ahead I said, "How'd you do on that test in Casey's class?"

Claire said, "What test?"

I tried to remember. How long ago had we taken it?

Claire tried to help me out. "Oh, that test. I did okay. How'd you do?"

"Okay." I really couldn't remember.

"You would. Everything's easy for you."

My neck thawed out, and I turned around. What gave her that idea?

"You're in the accelerated program aren't you?"

The school had put me in advanced English and advanced math, which was Algebra. "How'd you know that?"

"Because I have Algebra with you."

Of course. She sat in the back in first-hour Algebra, so I couldn't stare at her like I did in American History.

Mr. Richardson turned the car into the school's parking lot. I planned what I would do. The minute he stopped the car, I would reach over the seat and pop Claire's door open before she could.

And that's what I did. Except, by mistake, I locked it

instead. I fumbled with the handle, pushing it up and down, trying to get the door unlocked.

"I'll get it," Claire said.

At least I managed to shut the door for her after she got out. Maybe a little too hard, because her dad winced.

He leaned across the front seat and handed me the corsage. "I bet you didn't intend this for me." He pointed at his jacket and jeans. "It doesn't go with my ensemble."

"Thanks." I gripped the corsage box like it contained explosives. "Thanks for bringing us."

Mom had told me it was correct etiquette to pin Claire's corsage on her shoulder, but I had no intention of trying that since I couldn't even work a car door. When we were almost to the front door I said, "You want this?" and handed it to her.

She looked into the box. "Pretty," she said. "Thank you." Her smile made my legs melt.

Claire stopped at a table in the front hallway where the Home Ec. teacher, Mrs. Frost, was counting dollar bills into a small metal box.

"Claire," she said. "How pretty you look."

Claire got kind of flustered, glanced back at me, and pulled three dollars out of a change purse.

"You two have a nice time tonight." Mrs. Frost smiled.

The gym looked like a different place from the last time I'd been in it running laps in PE. Orange paper balls and white crepe paper hung overhead, and a spotlight on the floor beamed colored lights onto the ceiling. Card tables around the edges of the room had cornucopia decorations with artificial fruit spilling out.

"Cool decorations," I said. "You helped with this?"

"Honor Society did it." Her forehead wrinkled. "Why aren't you in Honor Society?"

"I think I got an invitation." I tried to remember what I'd done with it. "But maybe that was Chess Club."

Claire studied me like I had bugs on my face.

I wondered if people going crazy felt this—like a curtain had fallen and was keeping them from seeing parts of their life.

"Would you like to go sit down?"

She nodded.

I led the way. Claire waved at some girls, who waved back really hard. The guys with them turned around and gazed after Claire. I drew myself up so I'd be taller.

A deejay with hair past his shoulders was at the front of the gym. We'd just sat down when he put on "Born to Be Wild" at high volume.

"Wanna dance?" I said.

"Sure." Claire looked surprised. Most couples weren't dancing; they were standing in groups, the girls whispering together, the boys talking to each other.

I'd learned to dance watching Danny and his friends and their girlfriends at our house. If music came on when Danny and I were alone, he used to make me get up and follow his moves. Danny, no surprise, was a great dancer.

I held my hands in fists and moved my shoulders the way Danny had showed me, lifting first one, then the other. My feet moved without me telling them what to do. I didn't play an instrument like Danny did, and Dad had been pretty disappointed about that, but I'd inherited the musical gene. When music played, I wanted to move. Even though hardly anyone else was dancing, I didn't feel conspicuous.

Claire danced like she walked—sort of floated. She looked across at me and gave me the knec-melting smile.

74

In the doorway, Mrs. Frost and another teacher stood scowling. You could tell they didn't approve of the music.

"My dad hates this song," Claire yelled.

"If it were up to my dad," I hollered back, "stations would play only Bach and Mozart."

She nodded. "Nathan, too."

I reached out for her hands, and for a while we held hands as we danced. We danced that one, and the next one, and the next one. Claire smiled into space.

Slow dances terrified me, so when the deejay put one on, I started back to our table. Claire came along slowly, gazing back at the dance floor. She wanted to stay out there, but there were too many things about slow dancing I didn't understand—like how to stay off the girl's feet, and how to put your arm around her waist and hug her without seeming like you were hugging her.

"Do you go to basketball games?" I asked after we sat down. The season would be starting, and I could ask Claire to a game.

She shook her head.

"Don't you like them?"

She shrugged. "I don't know anything about basketball. We don't watch sports on TV. And my parents think schools waste too much money on sports."

"So does my dad. He gets pretty jealous of how much his school spends for football equipment compared to how much they spend on the music department. He teaches orchestra."

"My mom says the goal of schools should be to teach kids to think," Claire said. "She says, what good is school spirit and school loyalty when we get older?"

"Wow. Your mom sounds like my mom."

From where I sat, I could see Rick and Cindy at a

75

table, staring into space. I felt lucky to be with somebody easy to talk to.

Claire smiled at me. They were playing a fast one, and we jumped up to go dance.

We didn't stop dancing until the next slow song. I didn't have to lead Claire off the floor then—she was tired, and I followed her back to the table.

"So, how many brothers and sisters do you have?" she asked.

"One brother."

"Older or younger?"

"Older. Already graduated."

"Me too!" She flashed the great smile. "My older brother is graduated, and I have a younger brother."

My own face stretched with a grin. We sure had a lot in common. "There was just me and Danny, before he left."

"My older brother's not at home, either. He went to Canada to avoid the draft."

That's how she said it. Just that casual. Like it was no bigger deal than, "My brother likes cars."

I took a breath and asked, "And do you think that's right?"

She looked surprised. "Well, yeah. He doesn't want to risk his life over there."

"He's waiting it out in Canada while other American guys are getting killed?"

"Why should he risk his neck for something he doesn't believe in?"

"Freedom? He doesn't believe in freedom?"

She started to look kind of scared. She touched my arm and said, "Maybe this isn't something we should talk about. You must feel different about it—I guess you do, since you sent your dog over there."

"People should be loyal to their country when it's at war," I said.

Two kids at the next table turned around. Claire pulled a hunk of hair into her mouth.

After a minute, she pushed back her chair, and in the few seconds it took her to stand up, she transformed back into a cool, queenly person. "I'm going to go to the restroom, Mark." She glanced at the scoreboard clock. It was 7:45.

I sat there thumping my hand on the table and tapping my foot to the music. Something hot moved under my skin, wanting to bust out.

Claire didn't come back until 7:53. Her face looked red, like she'd washed it. "Want to dance one more? Then my dad will be here."

The words *Guess where* my *brother is?* were on the tip of my tongue. But I could see how hard Claire was trying. I said, "Sure."

* * *

When we walked out, three guys at the edge of the school yard were listening to loud music on a transistor radio and smoking. Claire's dad was waiting in the parking lot.

Claire crawled into the backseat, and I climbed in after her.

"Well, how was the dance?" Mr. Richardson asked, real hearty.

"Good," I said.

"We danced nearly every one." Claire's voice sounded back to normal.

"So, would you kids like to go have a malt?"

Claire looked at me and I saw a flash of worry.

"Sure," I said. I dug in my pants pocket to see if I'd remembered to bring the money Dad had given me. I relaxed when I felt it there.

Claire's dad drove to an ice-cream shop in the big shopping center a couple of miles from school. Our family didn't go there much because it was more expensive than the Dairy Queen five blocks from our house.

I fingered the dollars in my pocket. I could order just a Coke if things were too expensive.

But when he dropped us off, Mr. Richardson handed Claire a five-dollar bill.

"My dad gave me money," I said.

"This is girl's night to treat, I'm told," he said.

The menu had pictures of malts and sundaes and floats. Everything looked great. But I didn't order a malt because I might slurp it when I got to the end. A hot fudge sundae could be a mess. Anything with chocolate might end up on my shirt. So I ordered a dish of mint ice cream.

Claire ordered a banana split. That was okay for her, because girls were naturally dainty eaters.

"So, what's your favorite song?" she asked.

I hadn't been listening to music much lately because I had been writing letters and worrying about Wolfie and Danny. "Um, I like a lot of 'em. How about you?"

"'Dream a Little Dream of Me' by Mama Cass." Claire dribbled chocolate topping onto her sleeve.

"That's a good one."

"And 'Hey Jude.'" She had started on the strawberry sauce, and red goo dripped from her spoon onto the counter. "And 'Universal Sold—'" She stopped, and peeked up with a panicked look.

"Universal Soldier" was a peacenik song. But I acted like I hadn't heard and asked, "Which song does your dad hate most?"

"'In-A-Gadda-Da-Vida!'" She grinned from under a whipped-cream mustache. "When it comes on, he shuts off the radio."

I said, in a Dad-like voice. "There are no *lyrics.*"

Claire made her voice deep, too. "There's no *music,* either."

"Those idiots were *high* when they recorded it." I tried to scowl, but Claire and I were laughing.

* * *

At my house, I thanked Claire for asking me, and thanked her dad for driving us.

She said, "Thank you for the pretty corsage," in a dreamy voice.

"I'll see ya at school."

* * *

Mom was sitting in Dad's recliner, reading the paper. The big chair had swallowed her up, and she looked small and forlorn.

"Mark." She forced a smile. "How was the dance?"

"Good. Where's Dad?"

"A music teachers' association meeting. Want something to eat or drink?"

"I didn't finish the stew. I'd like the rest."

I still thought of Mom as bigger than me, but following her into the kitchen, it struck me that we were the same height.

"Your first real dance. Tell me about it."

I told her the story of riding in the front seat while

79

Claire rode in the back by herself. Mom smiled. I told her about wrestling with the car door, and locking it by mistake. Mom started to laugh. I told her about leaving the corsage on the seat. She really laughed.

It was like old times, with Mom laughing beside the counter while one of her boys told funny stories. But this time, Danny wasn't the star of the kitchen, I was.

9

I went to sleep with "Born to Be Wild" playing in my head and colored lights flashing behind my eyes, and Claire holding my hand and smiling.

When I got up the next morning, the kitchen smelled of bacon and pancakes, and Mom and Dad were sipping coffee.

"How many pancakes, Mark?" Mom asked.

"Four."

"You got a letter." Mom handed me an envelope.

I was surprised to see *Tucker Smalley and Wolfie* written on the return address. I'd received Tucker's first letter only a week before, and he couldn't have received the one I'd just sent. Which made me wonder why I'd gotten another letter so soon. As I pulled the letter out, Mom and Dad leaned toward me with worried frowns. I crawled up on a stool, the two of them watching me with hawk eyes.

I unfolded a wrinkled piece of spiral notebook paper. A picture fell out. I picked it up and saw a soldier in olive drab pants and shirt kneeling next to Wolfie. Wolfie had his head tilted like he was listening.

"Wolfie looks thin," I said.

Mom leaned over and looked. "Maybe they shaved him because of the heat down there. Heat and fleas."

I couldn't tell if that was the case. Dad held out his hand and I passed the picture to him.

"Nah, Mark, he's not skinny. He looks good. Look how his coat shines. They're brushing him a lot."

"Mark brushed him a lot," Mom said.

I gazed at Wolfie. The camera had given his eyes a red glare, but otherwise, it had caught the real dog—his alertness, his happiness, his gentleness.

After staring at Wolfie for a time, I started studying Tucker Smalley. He was nothing like I had pictured. I had thought he might look like the tough guys at Danny's high school or like a hillbilly, with a low forehead and goony expression. But Tucker had a nice face, blond hair, short, of course, and ruddy skin and freckles.

"Handsome young man," Mom said. "More serious than Danny."

"Isn't everybody?" I asked.

Tucker had his hand resting on Wolfie's neck. I would have liked it better if he'd had his arm around Wolfie, like he was pleased to have him. But if Tucker and the army didn't like Wolfie, that might be all the better for me getting him back. It might be foolish to hope, but I couldn't help it.

Dear Mark,

It's busy here. We been training the dogs on obstaculs and it's hard work and I don't mean just for the dogs. I also been doing a lot of paper work to get ready to go to 'Nam. Last week, a dog handler who done two tours over there come and talked to us. He told us stories about the dogs we couldn't hardly believe and how if it wasn't for them, guys would have been killed on the spot.

Tucker's buddy hadn't helped him this time. This letter had more mistakes than the first one.

He said the dogs are sometimes smarter than the man in charge. He told us about a dog and his handler who was leading a patrol. The dog alerted and the handler give the signal to stop, but the patrol leader said no, keep going, and the patrol walked right into a ambush and two soldiers was killed. The handler got injured and so did the dog. A helicopter come to take the handler out but the pilot didn't want to take the dog. The handler had to beg him. I bet I wouldn't beg. The pilot would be injured worse than me after I got done with him. HA!

Mom put pancakes in front of me, but I wasn't hungry anymore. I wished Mom and Dad would quit looking at me.

Some day I'm going to learn to spell. When I get back from 'Nam I'm going to elektrishan's school and the army will pay for it. Elektrishans have to know how to spell to run their business. The career officer said I will have to know math, too.

Ole Wolfie got the sarge POed the other day. We had started teaching the dogs to trail people. We put guys in a field and then ask the dogs to find them. The dogs like to do it, it's a game for them, and Wolfie done fine at first. But we was in the middle of the exercise and Wolfie spied a off-duty handler and his dog in the distance having a game of catch. Wolfie shot off to go play with them even though he had his working harness on. The sarge had a few choice words for Wolfie.

You can see I got my hands full trying to teach this dog life ain't all a party. But he done something the other day that showed he is pretty smart after all.

Some of us was playing Frisbee with our dogs. A couple of the dogs are amazing at it, and Wolfie is pretty good, too—loves to catch the Frisbee and bring it back to me.

Scoville, this black guy from Florida, didn't join in and play because he'd got a Dear John from his girl. He just sat there, reading the letter over and over. He was planning to marry the girl, but she told him she didn't want to wait for him and now she is going with Scoville's friend. If I was Scoville, I'd take leave and go have a serees talk with the so-called friend. He might not look so good to girls anymore. HA!

Anyway, Scoville was all busted up, sitting on top of a picnic table staring into space. The second time I throwed the Frisbee, Wolfie didn't bring it back to me. He run off and took it to Scoville. Scoville told him to go away. Wolfie put his paws up on the table and tried to make Scoville take it.

I called Wolfie back and throwed the Frisbee again. Wolfie done the same thing, took it to Scoville.

About the fourth time, Scoville just give up and got off the table and throwed the Frisbee for Wolfie. After a few times, he went over to the kennels and got his own dog and started playing with him. Wolfie had never

refused to bring the Frisbee back to me before, so I think
he somehow knew Scoville was sad and shouldn't be left
alone.
     Well, that's all for now.
               Tucker Smalley and Wolfie

Mom read the letter after I finished. "That's our Wolfie," she said, her face wistful.

"I wonder why I got another letter so soon."

"This kid is lonely. Maybe his family doesn't write much."

"Maybe they don't know how to write."

"Mark."

"Eve," Dad said, "we have illiterate people in this country, you know."

Mom sighed. "I'm putting together a package for Danny. Cookies and gum and notepaper and dried fruit. I'll make one up for Tucker, too."

"Your breakfast is getting cold, Mark," Dad said. "So, how was the dance?"

I blurted, "Claire's brother is a draft dodger."

Mom's eyebrows lifted.

Dad said, "How do you know?"

"She told me. She said it like it was nothing."

Dad put his coffee cup down. "This country is in sad, sad shape when people don't think it's a disgrace to have a draft dodger in the family. Did he go to Canada?"

"Yeah."

"I guess I don't have to ask how the dance was." Dad shook his head.

Mom worked her mouth like she was about to say something.

"What?" Dad said.

85

"Does that follow? That two kids can't have fun at a dance if their ideas don't agree?"

Dad rolled his eyes. "This isn't disagreeing over what kind of pizza to order. We are at war. In some countries, men get executed if they refuse military service."

"Not here, though." Mom stuck out her chin slightly. "We respect dissent, don't we?"

"That kid isn't dissenting, he's shirking. We make provisions for conscientious objectors. They work as medics, do paperwork, peel potatoes—they help in other ways. Guys don't need to be sitting it out in Canada, earning money and living it up, while other boys are in Vietnam."

Mom started gathering the breakfast things. Dad rubbed his lips together and nodded at me.

Mom turned around. "But if someone were against the war, why would he want to be over there helping?"

Dad said, "Boys can't just pick and choose which wars to be in. They have a job to do, to defend our country."

"A majority of people in this country don't see it that way."

Dad and I stared at Mom. Where had she gotten such a crazy idea?

Mom's chin fought to stay up. "The latest poll shows fifty-two percent don't believe we should be over there at all."

Dad huffed air out his teeth. "As though we can trust polls. Polls show whatever the pollster wants them to show." He scowled. "Eve, we have a son in Vietnam."

Mom's chin lost its battle to stay up. A minute later, she disappeared into a cloud of steam as she ran hot water on the breakfast plates.

Dad blew on his hands and rubbed them. "Mark, how long has it been since we've had a chess game?"

"Long time," I said, and followed him to the living room.

* * *

Dad hovered above the chess pieces, his eyebrows knotted over his nose. His faded green bathrobe smelled sweaty in a good way, and stubble shadowed his jaw. He didn't shave on Saturdays, at least not until afternoon. My fingers went up and tested my own chin. While Dad studied the board, I studied the shiny place on his balding head.

He beat me, as usual, but I think I surprised him with a couple of good moves.

Dad went off to get dressed; I went into the kitchen, where Mom was measuring ingredients for banana bread. She glanced over her shoulder as she filled a teaspoon with salt.

I took a deep breath, so my voice wouldn't jump. "I'm not sorry I sent Wolfie."

Mom emptied the teaspoon into the bowl, turned around, and looked at me. "I thought you were feeling kind of sorry."

"No!"

Her head moved in an up and down motion, then she picked up a big spoon and started to stir.

"I'm not going to turn traitor."

Her eyes pulled into a squint. "Okay."

She said it so quietly, I understood it only by reading her lips.

10

Rick peered up at the clouds above his house. "Looks like rain. Let's walk."

"We could get wet."

"Okay, then let's run." He bolted off.

I dashed after him. Small drops started to ping onto the sidewalk.

By the time we got to the A&W, Rick was a half block ahead. No wonder he was so good at basketball.

When we got our floats, I stirred all the ice cream into the root beer to make the whole thing foamy before I took my first sip. "I wrote Tucker, Wolfie's handler, and asked him how long dogs have to stay in Vietnam."

"What'd he say?"

"Haven't heard back yet."

"Did you ask him how many war dogs get killed in action?"

Root beer went bitter in my throat. "I didn't think to ask him that." What I meant was, even though Rick was my best friend, I didn't think it was too cool of him to bring that up.

When we got back to Rick's house, a white van with the words MOUNTAIN VIEW DRY CLEANERS was parked in the driveway. Rick's dad ran a dry cleaning business and he was hardly ever home. I'd only seen him a half-dozen times in all the years I'd known Rick.

"Uh-oh," Rick said. "Dad's here. I better split."

He didn't invite me in.

* * *

After school on Monday, Mom called to say the library had changed her hours and now she wouldn't get home until seven every night. She seemed really excited. "They want me to be here during the busiest hours, when kids are working on research projects and people are stopping on their way home from work."

"What about dinner?" I opened the fridge and saw that we were covered for that night. A meatloaf sat on the second shelf.

"You and Dad can have the snacks I've been making. I leave plenty, don't I? Or, I guess you could go ahead and eat without me."

"Uh-huh." Pretty soon she'd be working until eight and then nine, and then she'd be as tired as Dad when he came home, and we'd never get to talk at all.

* * *

After school on Tuesday, I went over to Effie's. When she opened the door and saw it was me, she clapped her hands. "Mark! So good to see you. Come in and have something to eat?"

"Well . . ."

She grabbed my arm and pulled me inside. "I have something . . ." She lifted her eyebrows up and down.

89

"What kind of streusel do you think I have baked?"

I'd had peach, apple, and blueberry streusel at her house. I tried to look thoughtful. "Broccoli?"

She frowned. "I didn't know anyone makes such a thing. It sounds not so—" Then she stopped, and pushed her head forward. "You are bad boy; shame on you! Go wash your hands and sit down."

After she had served me a helping of streusel and poured me a cup of hot tea from a blue-and-white pot, I gave her Tucker's most recent letter to read. When she came to the place where Tucker told about Wolfie trying to comfort the guy who got a Dear John letter, Effie shook her head. "Ach, how do dogs such things know?"

* * *

Next day in fourth hour, I watched Claire take out her notebook and carefully remove a couple of pieces of paper. The overhead light made red streaks in her dark hair.

Shouldn't she be ashamed of her brother? Someone so smart ought to care more about patriotism.

I tore a piece of notepaper out of my notebook and wrote on it,

There once was a girl named Claire
Who had long, beautiful hair.

I scrawled a line through the words. Sounded like I was in love or something. I started over.

There once was a girl named Claire
Who smelled like an old dead bear.

I scratched that out, too. Sounded like something Greg, Rick's little brother would write.

There once was a girl named Claire
Who thought the world was unfair
Because boys went to war,
Without knowing what for.
She wanted love and peace everywhere.

The last line didn't come out how I meant it to. I'd meant to make her sound dumb. I wadded up the page and did an overhand toss to the wastebasket, three rows from where I sat. I didn't expect it to make it, and then Mr. Casey would ask me to come pick it up, but, to my surprise, the wad plopped right into the center of the basket. *So there, Claire.*

She was watching me. She had her arm over an open book, her knees pointed toward the aisle. She had that cool expression of hers, but she lifted her thumb and gave me the Claire smile.

* * *

I didn't expect anything in the mail because I'd just gotten a letter from Tucker the Friday before. But the mailbox held a letter addressed to me in Tucker's awful scrawl. This time, the return address didn't say *Tucker and Wolfie*, it said just *Wolfie*.

I ran into the house and ripped it open, and stood beside the counter reading it with my jacket still on.

Dear Mark,
Woof! I got lots of news.
You know how Tucker said I don't always keep my

mind on what's going on? Well, today I got something to brag on.

Sgt. Begay had us do a exercise that was hard. We had to go up in a helicopter and rappel out. We had harnesses on, and ropes, but it's still a lot like stepping out into thin air.

Sarge said us dogs usually like copters once we get used to the noise, but don't like being lowered out of one. So he went up with all of us, in groups of three or four dogs and their handlers.

Me and Tucker was in the third group. Tucker wasn't all that shiny about riding in a copter. The first plane he ever rode in was to get here, and he didn't think much of that, either, but at least the plane had walls and wasn't open to the sky.

A dog named Benny whined and tried to get off the copter when it started. Sarge told Benny's handler, Conrad, to kneel down and talk to him. Conrad had to hold Benny when the copter lifted off because Benny was trying to escape.

We flew over the trees and seen a river below, with boats and people fishing. Tucker and another guy said that made them homesick. Tucker looked sick, but the other kind of sick.

When we got to a open field, Sarge says, "Who's first?" Leland, this guy from Utah, said he'd go. Leland coaxed his dog to the door. "Let's go, Ranger." Ranger had on a harness made from a poncho. A soldier helped lower Ranger out the door. Ranger was whimpering and trying to hold onto the rope with his paws. Leland went next, talking to Ranger all the time, and then Ranger felt a little better because he wasn't hanging there by hisself.

Benny was cowering in a corner by then, because he could see that he'd have to do it. Conrad tried to tug him to the door, but Sarge told him the dog might yank him off balance. It took Sarge and another guy to lower Benny out the door. Benny yelped like he was in mortal agony.

When Sarge looked my way, that's all it took. I run to the door, and they couldn't get me rigged fast enough. When they lowered me out, I floated there happy as a pig in the sunshine, a big smile on my face. It didn't scare me a bit. Tucker come next, not near as happy about it as me.

Sarge said he'd never seen a dog so willing on a first time. It changed his mind about me. He said in 'Nam dogs have to put up with heat, humidity, bugs, rain, mud, and stress, and a dog with a great attitood like mine would be a asset. Sarge had been thinking of holding me back for more training, but now he says Tucker and me will ship out with the others. They need dogs bad, so guess when we are leaving? Eight days! Ain't that a surprise?

You can stik out your chest about me being star of the class today. I know you must be proud and happy because I was your dog first.

I don't know where we're going and neither does Tucker. I will write when I get there. Tell your naybor I wouldn't mind more of them homemade treats and Tucker wouldn't turn down your Mom's snikerdooduls. HA!

Love,
Wolfie

PS Tucker says to tell you the answer is yes about the

bounty. The VC have put out a reward for killing dogs and handlers. The killer gets a reward when he turns in the dog's tattooed ear or the handler's patch from his shirt. Scuse me, I gotta scratch my ear, this talk is making me itch. HA!

I tore out of the house, jumped on my bike, and pedaled down the street.

11

I looked through the glass library doors and the first person I saw, sitting on the rug cross-legged with a bunch of little kids, was Mom. She was holding up a picture book and pointing to something on the page. A little girl in a blue dress was sitting in Mom's lap.

I stood in the red tile lobby surrounded by a jungle of potted plants and watched her. In the months Mom had worked there, I'd only gone to see her once, and that had been Rick's idea. We were riding past on our bikes and Rick said, "Let's go see your mom." That day she was helping to check out books for a long line of people, so we didn't talk to her.

After the little kids went off with their mothers, I went over to her.

"Mark, what are you doing here?" She looked really happy to see me.

"I didn't know you read to little kids."

"We take turns. We nearly come to blows over who gets to do it."

"You never mentioned it."

"I don't remember anyone at home ever asking me about my job." She said it nonchalantly, like that didn't annoy her, but I think it did.

"What brings you here?" Then she must have noticed my worried face, because all of a sudden her hands pulled into fists and the fists came up and pushed against her chest.

I couldn't get the words out fast enough. "It's nothing about Danny."

She closed her eyes and huffed out air. "Thank God."

Another librarian standing across the room was watching her with a worried look.

"Are you okay?" I asked.

She nodded, her shoulders sagging. "I shouldn't jump to conclusions. You could have come to say the oven wasn't working. I don't have to assume . . ." Her voice sounded like she'd been inhaling helium balloons.

"They're sending Wolfie to Vietnam."

"Oh." I don't think she heard because she was still recovering from her scare. I felt my neck tighten with anger. I understood that she was acting like any mother of a soldier would, but still, Danny had managed to shove me aside even when I had big, terrible news.

"Oh!" She came back to her body. "Oh, Wolfie. When did you find out? What about him being held back for more training?" She looked at me. "This is bad news, right? Or . . . is it?"

"Yeah!"

"But, you want him to be over there helping? You said . . ." She stopped and laid her hand on my arm.

I stared at the tiles until the lines on them got hazy. Feeling mad had been easier. I didn't want Mom to be too

96

nice, not here in the library in front of everyone.

She must have read my mind because she took back her hand and said in a crisp, librarian voice, "I'm glad you came over to tell me. When I get home tonight, I want the details. Are you going back home now?"

I shrugged.

"Go next door and see Effie."

I shook my head.

"Run some errands at the store for me?"

I nodded, not wanting to talk right then because I might have a helium voice, too.

Mom handed me some money and named three or four items she wanted. "Go to Safeway, if you don't mind."

"Okay." She probably understood I didn't want to see Mr. Sevorn at the A&P because he would ask about Danny and Wolfie.

"I'm due for a break. I'll walk you outside." Mom tugged on my shirt.

A short woman with curly gray hair wheeling a cart of books smiled at Mom and me and stopped the cart in our path. The books smelled old.

"This must be your boy, Eve."

"Yes, this is Mark. Mark, meet Mrs. Peters, Jackie Peters."

The woman extended her hand.

"Nice to meet you," I said.

"You're the one who sent his dog to the army."

Of all subjects to bring up. My eyes traveled to the glass double doors. There must be a way to get to them without seeming too conspicuous.

I took a sideways step to move around the cart.

"Did your mom give you the article?"

Mom shook her head at the woman, but the woman was looking at me.

"Article?" I asked.

"The one from the *Chicago Tribune* about the dogs in Vietnam. Fascinating, but it's—" She stopped when she caught Mom's warning scowl.

Mom stepped around the cart, pulled on my elbow, and said, "I'll be right back, Jackie; just going to walk Mark out."

Mrs. Peters nibbled her bottom lip.

"What article?" I asked. "Can I see it?"

"Some other time, Mark. Today wouldn't be good."

I pulled my elbow loose. "Why?"

"You've had enough for one day."

Something told me that was true, but on the other hand, I didn't want her making that decision for me.

"Where is it?"

Mom stopped. "Trust me, Mark, today isn't—"

"Where is it?"

She turned and I followed her to the reference desk. She reached under the counter and brought out a fat newspaper. "I haven't had a chance to make a copy yet. Anyway, it might be better if you read it here." She pointed to an empty table with four empty blue chairs. "Bring it back when you're done. I want to know what you think of it."

I spread out the paper. On the front page, I saw what had drawn Mom's attention. DOGS FACE UNCERTAIN FUTURE, it said. Under that, in smaller print, it said, "The *Tribune's* Vietnam correspondent Eddie Taylor reports that the army's vague policy toward canine soldiers has dog handlers worried. Sec C-4."

"I'll be at the front desk," Mom said. I sat down at a table and turned to the story.

Saigon, South Vietnam

When Pfc. Ronnie Lorenzo returns home to Dearborn, Michigan, he will meet his six-month-old daughter, Kimberly, for the first time. He looks forward to sharing McDonald's french fries with his wife, Tammy, and rebuilding the engine in his '59 'Vette. But Lorenzo's enthusiasm about going home is dampened by worries about leaving his companion, Shadow, a six-year-old German shepherd scout dog.

"I wouldn't be going home alive if it weren't for Shadow," Lorenzo said. "He saved my life more than once. He took a bullet in his leg two months ago because he was walking ahead of me. It was a bullet I would have caught."

Shadow has been in Vietnam for three years and has been wounded three times, once so seriously that the camp veterinarian doubted he would pull through. But he did, and was returned to duty. During his career, Shadow has saved his fellow soldiers by detecting trip wires, *punji* sticks, snipers, ambushes, and snakes. Lorenzo thinks it is time that the army rewards Shadow by letting him return to normal life. Lorenzo has been writing letters to the army, asking that Shadow be allowed to go home with him when he leaves in December.

So far, Lorenzo's efforts have met with frustration. He has not been able to work his way through a maze of army bureaucracy and obfuscation. "They keep stalling," Lorenzo said. "They say quarantine issues must be considered, and also the shortage of dogs. When they said that dogs fall under the designation 'army equipment,' I went nuts."

Scout dogs sniff out an area before patrols go in. Lorenzo, who trained at Fort Benning, Georgia, inherited Shadow when he arrived in Vietnam last December. "You don't always get a Christmas present that will save your life," he said.

Lorenzo was told that Shadow was a one-man dog and had been bonded with his former handler, Pfc. Jerry Hernandez. "They said Hernandez bawled like a kid when he said good-bye to Shadow. Everybody worried that Shadow wouldn't take to a new handler. I worked really hard to get him to like me. After a couple of weeks, he came around, and has been my best friend since."

Lorenzo's family in Dearborn have become experts on the army's policy regarding dogs following the end of World War II. Some military brass worried then that dogs would be unable to adjust to civilian life, that they, like some soldiers, were shell-shocked. But the military successfully rehabilitated the dogs, which returned to the U.S. to live peacefully in civilian families.

"Only a few dogs, I mean a handful, weren't able to be rehabilitated and returned to civilian life. I know Shadow would do great," Lorenzo said.

Erratic weather, illness, and enemy raids have made soldiers edgy and argumentative with each other at Lorenzo's camp. But the men agree on one issue—that Shadow should be allowed to retire and go back to the U.S. Some soldiers have joined Lorenzo in writing letters on Shadow's behalf.

Many servicemen in Vietnam acknowledge that they owe their lives to the alert actions of a scout or sentry dog, according to Capt. Les Couch, a veterinarian who has treated canine battle wounds and jungle-related diseases. "These dogs are the greatest. On top of saving lives, they

100

provide—this may sound strange—some humanity for their units."

Three kinds of dogs are being used in country: scout, sentry, and tracking. Sentry dogs patrol the periphery of camps and bases, guarding soldiers from attack and equipment from theft. Tracking dogs, which are few in number, pursue enemy troops and locate wounded U.S. soldiers.

Scout dogs, especially, share everyday routines and hardships with their handlers. A handler packs his dog's rations along with his own.

"They once sent out awful dog food that Shadow wouldn't touch, so I shared my rations with him. A bunch of other guys insisted on sharing theirs, too. We were kind of low on supplies, but they wanted to do it. Shadow was on human rations for almost a month, not that they are anything to brag about."

Lorenzo worries that Shadow's luck may run out before he gets his deserved rest. He fears that the next time Shadow gets hurt in the line of duty or contracts a jungle illness, he may not pull through.

Lt. Col. William P. Gillian, commander of the 2nd Battalion, 1-16 Infantry, declined commenting on Lorenzo's request. "The army has many issues to consider," he said.

Lorenzo says he feels frustrated and angry about how the war is being run. "But that is nothing to what I'll feel if I can't take Shadow out with me."

Next to the article was a picture of Lorenzo with a big black German shepherd. The dog was standing on his hind legs with his paws on Lorenzo's shoulders. Lorenzo was looking at the camera and the dog was looking at him, his long nose almost touching Lorenzo's.

I didn't shut the paper, didn't take it back to Mom. I

got up and hurried out of the library and down the sidewalk, crossed the street, and started walking. Then I broke into a run. I ran past the A&P, past the drugstore, past the vacant lot where Rick and I used to build roads in the dirt and run toy tanks. My chest was heaving and I had a stitch in my side, but I kept going.

I don't know how long I wandered around, but when I went home and walked in the back door, Dad was waiting. "Hey," he said real hearty, but he looked all worn out. "Your mom's been calling. Worried about you. But you're okay, huh?"

I knew he wanted me to say yes. "Yes."

"So, we'll have two soldiers from this family in Vietnam?" He lifted his fist and winked. "I told your mom, of course you would feel worried about Wolfie, but you knew going in where he was headed. She thinks you're upset and—"

"I'm going to my room," I said. I hardly ever cut Dad off, so he didn't follow.

I took the sack from my closet and sat down on the bed. The first thing I pulled out was a homemade toy, a dog chew I'd braided out of lake weed one year at summer camp. I'd missed Wolfie so much that whenever we did a craft project, I'd make something for him. He destroyed most of them as soon as I gave them to him, but the toy I'd made from lake weed had survived a lot of use.

I ran Wolfie's dog brush over the bedspread. When I brushed Wolfie, he would close his eyes. Danny said he went into an altered state like hippies do with drugs. I'd never been able to brush him as much as he craved. One time I'd tried to see how long I could last, and Wolfie still looked like he was in heaven after an hour, but my hand had gone numb.

The brush had been a present from Effie. Its handle was painted blue and red and it had stiff bristles that never wore down. Mom had brought it in out of the weather even when I forgot, so it still looked good.

Mom tapped on the door. I hadn't even heard her come home. "Honey, it's dinnertime."

"I'm not hungry."

"Can I come in?"

When I didn't answer, she opened the door a crack. "Are you okay?"

"I don't want to talk about Wolfie."

"Okay." She started to sit down on the edge of the bed, but I bounced up and out of the room and went to the dinner table. Dad must have seen something in my face, because he talked all through dinner about how the music budget for orchestra had been cut again.

12

"Is my lunch ready?" I asked.

Mom glanced up at the clock. "Almost."

"Could you hurry and finish it?"

Mom placed items in a sack. "Tuna sandwich, an orange, celery sticks, the last brownie, milk money. That ought to hold you. You don't need to leave so early, do you?"

"Yeah."

She waited for me to say more, but I couldn't explain why I was taking off a half hour early. All I knew was, when I woke up that morning, I had an irresistible urge to go to the park before school.

Effie already was out sweeping her walk. She swept her front porch and sidewalk every morning. By itself that wasn't so weird, but she'd be back out by four that afternoon, doing it all again. How dirty could a sidewalk get in that amount of time?

Effie fluttered her hand. "How are you . . . Marcaroni?" Her voice held a giggle.

"Okay."

"You have not been to my house for a long time."

She always said that, even if you'd just been over.

She called, "Any news from Danny?"

"Nothing new." Mom called Effie the minute she got a letter from Danny, and Effie knew that. And it wasn't like we got lots of letters from him.

I turned up the collar on my jacket and drove my hands into my pockets. The day was sunny and Effie looked comfortable in her old black sweater, but my skin tingled in the sharp breeze.

Had I always been so jealous of Danny? I tried to remember what typical times used to be like around our house.

The picture I came up with was supper one evening, with Mom standing at the stove filling bowls of soup, Dad looking tired from school, and Danny, lips twisted, talking in a strangled voice, imitating his World History teacher.

Mom turned around, trying to look stern, but you could tell she was about to bust. Dad, who had every reason to disapprove of poking fun at teachers, leaned his head on his arm, hiding a smile. I couldn't see myself in the picture, though I knew I was there. Invisible, I guess. I tried to remember what I was thinking or feeling at the time, but couldn't.

When I turned the corner, a gust carrying leaves and dust blew into my face. I ducked my head and crossed the street, heading for the park.

It wasn't quite true that I couldn't remember how I'd felt, sitting there like a bump on a log at the dinner table. I had wanted to yell, "He's not the only kid in the family!" I didn't, of course, because jealousy wasn't a proper thing to feel.

I sat down on top of a picnic table. The wood felt cold on my butt and a sour smell came from the leaves blanketing the grass. Two fat women in sweat suits came by, not sweating one bit. They were walking so slow a turtle could have passed them.

Danny used to say it was me who got special treatment from Mom and Dad, because he never got to have a dog. I think Mom and Dad let me have Wolfie because a dog wouldn't be any more trouble than the animals I'd been dragging home: a squirrel that had been hit by a car, a mouse injured in Effie's trap, a baby robin that fell from a tree.

I had to make all the promises parents insist on when a kid gets a dog. I promised to clean up after him, feed, water, and brush him. I forgot sometimes—well, quite a few times actually—and Mom did it. But she made me clean up after him in the yard and sweep up when he tracked mud in the house.

I picked up a rock from the ground and hurled it at the wooden park sign. "Damned army!" I yelled. A woman pushing a little kid in a swing turned and looked at me.

I sat down on a bench, pulled out a notebook and wrote:

A kid named Mark from the West
Thought that the army knew best.
But when Mark looked around,
Mass confusion he found.
"I made a mistake," he confessed.

I crossed out the last line. I had done a good thing. Patriotic. Unselfish.

I wadded up the paper and threw it on the ground.

No dogs were at the park. Usually, someone was there walking a dog or playing fetch, but not today. People with dogs should have been at the park playing with them. It wasn't that cold.

* * *

When I got to school, the first person I saw was Claire. She was moving down the hall by herself, or maybe it only seemed that way because she was taller than her friends. A crush of kids carried her off, but she gazed back at me, smiling. I ran my hand over my wind-blown hair.

No one else had a jacket on. I tried to find a clock, and when I did, I stared at it, mouth hanging. I'd missed first period altogether, and kids already were changing classes.

I ran to my locker and stuffed my coat in it. I picked up my books and sprinted to my second-hour class. Already the halls were emptying, and I was close to being late.

I dashed into my second-hour class just as the bell rang. The teacher had her back turned, so I zipped to my seat and plunked down before she turned around.

In fourth hour, I looked straight at the board so that I wouldn't give in to a temptation to look at Claire. I wondered if she was looking at me. If so, she would see the neat arrangement I'd made on my desk—my notebook and two textbooks in an even line, with two ballpoints placed on either side, perfectly level with each other.

"Answer questions one through ten at the end of the chapter," Mr. Casey was saying.

I opened my history book. A hand touched my shoulder. "Can I see you in the hall for a minute?"

I looked up at Mr. Casey, and nodded.

"No talking," he called over his shoulder.

He came right to the point. "I heard you missed Honors Algebra," he said.

I stared at him.

"I heard in the teachers' lounge."

"They talk about me?"

"First hour is an accelerated class. Miss Thompson notices when a student isn't doing well."

"This is the first time I've missed her class."

"You're flunking in there. And close to flunking my class."

"Flunking?" How could that be? I was a pretty good student.

"These are core classes, Mark. If you don't pull your grades up, you'll be held back. That'd be a shame for someone as bright as you."

I stared at the floor tiles, feeling unconnected to the conversation. Flunking? I hadn't paid much attention to the grades I'd gotten on papers. Maybe I'd forgotten to turn papers in. Maybe I hadn't done them at all.

Suddenly, the numbness went away. "You going to call my folks?"

"It's customary."

"Don't do that!"

Mr. Casey looked at me hard. "Come see me after school."

"Okay."

* * *

Mr. Casey had his long legs up on his desk and was gazing at the fluorescent ceiling lights and clicking a pen. He smiled when I walked in, and pointed to a chair.

"You didn't have a note to explain your absence this morning."

"No." I plunked my stuff down on top of a desk.

"How's Wolfie?"

My pulse came to a stop. But I was glad that he'd asked about him. "He and his handler, Tucker, are shipping out to Vietnam."

"Last time I talked to you, he wasn't doing well in training."

"Last week they were mad at him because he ran off to play during training. But then he did good rappelling out of a helicopter, and now they like him."

"Dogs rappel out of copters? That's hard to picture. So it doesn't look promising on getting him back?"

"It looks bad. He's army property now. That's what they told me."

"What does that mean for his future?"

My stomach got so tight it hurt.

"I mean, what about after he's served in Vietnam?"

I knew what he meant. "My mom found this article about a guy who is trying to bring his dog home with him from Vietnam. The dog has been there three years, but it sounded like the army wasn't going to let the dog go."

Mr. Casey winced. "Ouch."

"I wish I could just go down there and bust him out," I mumbled.

"It's worth a try."

I laughed out loud. You had to like a guy—an adult, I mean—who would consider such a thing.

He kept looking at me.

"Oh, sure. A kid against the army. How would I sneak onto an army base where everybody has M16s and tanks? How would I find the kennels?"

"Don't laugh," he said, just as serious as when he said, "No talking" in class.

I laughed anyway. "First thing, how would I even get there?"

"There may be another way to bust him out."

"Like?"

"Like, get someone on your side. A congressman, a dog club, a newspaper reporter. A journalist probably would go for a story about a boy and a dog."

"I wouldn't know what to say."

"Tell them you changed your mind and now you want your dog back."

"I want my dog back, but I haven't changed my mind."

"I don't understand."

"People have to make sacrifices for our country."

"Okay. Then what's the problem?"

"Dogs ought to be able to come home after they've served over there, just like soldiers do."

"So, that's what you tell them."

"Who?"

"Whoever it is you're trying to get on your side."

"It's too late to stop Wolfie from going to Vietnam."

"Yes. But if you start now, you may be able to bring him home after he's served a reasonable time."

"A reasonable time," I repeated. The hand on the clock clicked as it moved. "Where would I find out for sure about war dogs and if they get to come home? I wrote Tucker and asked him, but he hasn't answered yet."

"He may not have the answer. You may have to go higher."

"If they don't plan to give him back, can I complain?"

"Absolutely. You didn't understand how it worked, and that's your loophole."

"I didn't ask them."

"They could have volunteered that information. Should have."

"What do I do next?"

"Round up all the facts you can, then take action. Go out and talk to groups, like the Humane Society—"

"No!" Danny could have done that, but not me.

"—or write letters."

I wrote good letters. "I wouldn't know how to write my congressman."

"It's simple. You need extra credit in here, and that could earn you some. It probably would have to be more than one letter. One to the Department of the Army, and one to the people in charge of the program at Fort Benning. Be prepared to take it to a higher court if that doesn't work."

"Who? The president?"

"That's not out of the question, but I was thinking of the public. Everyone likes dogs. Get the people behind you."

He pointed at the portrait of Lincoln hanging above his desk and the banner with the words *Government of the people, by the people, for the people*.

I peered up at it.

He misread my silence.

"Our faith in government can falter, but we must keep believing in the principles this country was founded on."

He was talking about himself. I didn't have an opinion one way or the other about government. My dad complained about taxes and Mom complained that the city

111

should fix the potholes in our street, but government didn't have much to do with me.

"What made your faith falter?" I asked.

"I can't talk about it." Then, almost at once he said, "I guess I could, if it's just between us."

I nodded.

"I was called in by the school board, reported, I suppose, by other teachers, for challenging my students to think about whether it is right that we are in Vietnam. It's too complicated to explain quickly, but I believe we didn't follow our own rules in the way we got there. The school board told me to stop speaking against the war in class or lose my job. It doesn't seem democratic to me that I can't raise these issues, while pro-war teachers are able to speak their views."

I studied the rip in my left tennis shoe, which had gotten bigger. Dad would say no one had the right to criticize when we were at war because it was unpatriotic. Mom might say the school board had been unfair to Mr. Casey. I wished I knew which was right.

I stood up and put on my jacket. "Are you going to call my folks about my grades?"

"Your family has a lot on its mind right now. If you commit to doing your work in here, your grade can be between us." He waited.

"Okay." I didn't want to give my parents trouble right now. "I guess Miss Thompson will call them."

"Talk to her."

I nodded.

He said, kind of cagey, "I have some influence with her."

I narrowed my eyes at him. The eighth-grade girls would be heartbroken if they thought Mr. Casey had something going with Miss Thompson. Miss Thompson was really, really fine.

"Don't get your hopes up about this. The army is a huge bureaucracy."

I nodded.

"On the other hand, don't be surprised if this gets bigger than you expect. These are volatile times."

13

I called Mom from school before going over to the library, because I remembered how much it had scared her when I'd showed up there before. It might have scared her anyway when the person who answered the phone hollered, "Eve, your boy's on the phone." When Mom came on, she said, "Yes?" in a faraway voice.

"I'm doing some extra-credit work. If I come over, can you help me?"

"Yes."

"I'll be right down."

I found her in the magazine area, taking down old ones and putting up new ones. I'd only been to see her three times, but it seemed to me Mom worked harder than the others.

She smiled when she saw me. Beamed, really.

"What can I help you with?"

"I need the addresses of our congressman and also our senators."

"I'll show you where to get them."

114

She led me to an old-fashioned desk in the middle of the reading area. The desk held a stack of fat, leather-bound books. She pointed at one.

"The addresses will be in there, under *Colorado*, of course."

"Um, would the Department of the Army be there, too?"

"No." Her brows lifted. "Who do you want to reach at the army?"

"Whoever is in charge of the dogs."

Her head went up and down. "About Wolfie."

"Yeah."

"Want to say more?"

"I'm going to try and get him home after he serves a hitch. Like the other soldiers."

"Seems fair."

"That wouldn't make him a draft dodger."

"Especially since they don't draft dogs."

I heard a bite in her words. She had encouraged me to think twice about sending Wolfie. Or, maybe I was just prickly and imagined it.

Maybe the whole mess was my fault and I didn't have a leg to stand on with the army. Maybe they'd think I was just a whiner. I should have asked more questions before signing Wolfie up. But Mr. Casey was right, too, that the army should have told me more. I hoped I could make it up to Wolfie and fix it so he wouldn't have to stay too long.

Mom was paging through a different fat book. "Here are four pages in tiny print with army addresses. I suggest you call down to Fort Benning and find out who in Washington is in charge of the army dogs."

"Okay."

"Anyone else you want to write to?"

Mr. Casey had suggested that I might contact a reporter, but I had no interest in that. I wanted this to stay private. "That's it," I said.

"Let me know if I can be of any more help."

"Thanks," I said.

Back at home, I started the letter with "Dear Sir." I meant to keep it short, but ended up telling the whole story of how I'd found Wolfie at the animal shelter, how fat and silly he was as a puppy, and how friendly and kind he grew up to be. I realized halfway through the letter that I'd made Wolfie sound like an angel dog, and that wasn't true, so I told about some of his bad habits, like how he would sneak an entire cube of butter off the counter and lick his muzzle and smile after he'd swallowed it, even though he knew a scolding was coming—and how awful it was to clean up after him when he got sick and puked butter on the rug. Mom, Dad, and I still put the butter in the cupboard after we used it, out of habit.

I explained that when I'd donated Wolfie I didn't know he would become army "equipment." Equipment couldn't give love, and anyone who'd ever had a faithful dog knew no creature on the planet loved more than a dog did. I said I thought it would be fair if Wolfie served a hitch and then was sent home to me. While I was at it, I told them the other dogs serving in Vietnam ought to be able to come home, too.

The letter turned out to be seven notebook pages long. I would ask Mom to make copies for me at the library. I addressed all the envelopes right then.

By the time I came out of my room, I felt like I'd done something big. I carried the letter with me, hoping Mom or Dad would ask about it.

"Your letter done?" That from Mom.

"Who are you writing to?" Dad asked.

I traded a look with Mom. "The army, about Wolfie."

I let the pages slip from my fingers onto the coffee table. I went to the kitchen to get some milk, looking over my shoulder to see what happened with the letter. Mom picked it up, read it through, and when I came back she looked up, eyes blinking. "This is wonderful. Wonderful." Her voice sounded like sandpaper.

She handed the letter to Dad. He read it, nodding. A couple of times he smiled. After he finished it, he looked over at me. Not exactly at me. In my direction, but his eyes went somewhere behind me, to the wall. "Interesting, Mark."

"What does that mean?"

"You're quite the writer." He bounced his head, then picked up a book from the floor next to his recliner and started reading.

He was only three or four feet from me, but it felt like miles.

I could see Mom felt uneasy with his reaction. She stood, looked at me, then at Dad, and kind of sang, "What kind of cookies would everyone like? I'm in a baking mood."

"Sugar cookies? We haven't had them for a while." I looked at Dad to see what he thought.

"Um-hum, um-hum." He nodded.

"No need to hide the butter when I'm making them." Mom's voice still had a tune in it, but her smile was mournful.

∗ ∗ ∗

We got a letter from Danny.

117

Dear Mom, Dad, and Marcaroon,

Would you send me the addresses of the guys in the Invincible Tulip, at least Bill and Tony's? I've been listening to music they should hook into. It's a bigger world out here than any of us knew. This music is way out. Maybe the Denver stations don't air it, but I can tell them where to find it.

Thanks, Mom, for the paper, the paperback books, the cookies and all. I was nearly all out, and I appreciate it.

Tell Effie thanks for the great cookies. What? You're saying I should write her myself, Mom? Okay, I'll try. But in case I forget . . ."

"Short," Mom said about the letter.

"That's our Danny." But Dad looked disappointed. He held up the piece of notepaper with two fingers. "Nothing about the war."

"How does he use up the paper? Not by writing to us." Mom took the page from Dad, folded it, and put it back into the envelope.

"I don't know how the new music he likes could be any noisier than what they used to play. I'm surprised he can hear at all," Dad said.

"He didn't say it was louder. Just . . ." Mom fidgeted.

Dad waited.

"Wilder, maybe. Maybe political."

Dad got kind of a smirk. "Protest music?"

"Could be."

"Eve?" Dad smiled. "Danny is a soldier."

* * *

The first of my replies came by phone. I'd barely

118

gotten home from school when the phone rang and a woman said, "I'm calling for Mark Cantrell, please. This is Congressman Nelson's office."

It had been only a few days since I'd mailed the letters, and I wasn't expecting to hear so soon.

I didn't know a call could make me so scared. I wanted to say I wasn't home yet and call back later, but that would have required too many words. I forced out, "I'm Mark."

"Mark!" She made it sound like she'd reached the president or the queen of England. "Congressman Nelson asked me to call you and tell you how *much* he appreciated your letter. He read it with *great* interest and it went straight to his *heart.* The congressman and Mrs. Nelson can't have dogs where they live in Washington, but they have two cats they *adore,* so he is coming from the same place as *you* as far as being an animal lover."

My chest was hardly letting in any air, I was hoping so hard she was going to say something encouraging about Wolfie.

"Are your parents home, Mark?"

"No, they're both at work."

"Well, that's fine because it's *you* I wanted to talk to anyway." She said it so enthusiastically that I knew it was a lie.

"The congressman wants me to tell you three things. Mark?"

"Yeah."

"First, how *pleased* he is to see a young person step out and take an interest in government. He compliments you for understanding that it is a congressman's duty to care about the problems of his constituents. Second, he shares your concerns about the dogs who are serving in

Vietnam. He thanks you for making him aware of them. And third, he wants to commend you for sacrificing your beloved pet on behalf of the country." Her voice wasn't full of expression now, it sounded like she was reading the phone book. "Here are the congressman's words: 'We read and hear so much about the problems of today's youth— that they are lazy, self-indulgent, and tuned out. But a youngster like Mark makes us hopeful for a new generation that will lead our country to even greater heights.'"

I wasn't sure what that meant.

"Mark?"

"Yeah."

"Thanks again so much for your letter."

I couldn't let her hang up; I needed help for Wolfie. "What is the congressman going to do?" I asked.

I heard her take a breath. "Well . . . the congressman has been made aware of the situation, as I told you, and . . . he is committed to finding out more. I'm sure he'll be looking into . . . what status dogs have in the military, and what the army's policies are, specifically."

"And then he'll do something?"

"The congressman has the situation on his docket, and our office will contact you with any information we turn up."

"Thanks."

I wanted to be grateful that the congressman's office had called so quickly, but with all my heart I hoped I'd get better results from the others.

* * *

Dad said, "How about turning on the TV?"

Mom was at work until nine, getting ready for the library's used-book sale. She had made a big pot of spaghetti, and the house smelled of garlic and herbs. Mom had been making our favorite meals, maybe hoping that would help things get back to normal.

I thought Dad was more withdrawn than usual. Maybe he was worried about Danny; maybe he didn't like Mom working; maybe he thought my letters to the army meant I was joining the antiwar people. I hoped he would bring the subject up so I could tell him I was still loyal, but he didn't, and I didn't either.

When the picture came on, comedians Tommy and Dick Smothers were doing a routine.

"Change the channel," Dad said.

"Just a minute."

Dad used to like the Smothers Brothers, but he didn't anymore since they had become critical of the war. Their show had been canceled.

But tonight, they were guests on somebody else's show and doing their old routine, which consisted of Dick being smooth and smart and Tommy acting like a nitwit. Tommy had a line he would say to Dick that got lots of laughs: "M-mom always liked you better."

Tommy was stumbling through a tale about a family camping trip. He got confused, and Dick had to help him with the details. In the story, Tommy had put up the tent wrong and the ropes got tangled and the tent fell on people during the night and everything was a mess and their mother thought they'd never get it straightened out.

"See, see," Tommy said to his brother, his eyes really wide, "Mom, she, she always liked you better."

The laugh track went on forever. Dad laughed, too.

"Why is that so funny?" I asked.

"It's funny," Dad chuckled, "because every kid thinks

121

his mom loves his brother or sister more."

"Did you?"

Dad frowned. "I don't know. I was the only boy, and Mom seemed closer to my sisters, but—" He stopped. "Yeah. I thought Mom liked Janice and Marjorie better."

Dad reclined his chair. "How about you?"

I cracked my knuckles, frowning.

"I guess you'd have little reason to think that, with you and your mom being so much alike."

I stared at him.

"Quiet and thoughtful."

Was he serious? Had he forgotten how Mom and Danny used to have private jokes no one else was in on, and how Danny would make Mom laugh so hard she couldn't say anything and she'd have to wave at him to stop? Dad had to be blind.

* * *

It snowed a foot the next day, so I went to Effie's after school to shovel her walks. Dad, Danny, or I always did this during the winter.

Effie looked out her window and waved at me. She had a scarf on her silver hair and her nose looked red.

When I was finishing, she called, "Mark, come in for a minute." It would be the ritual I knew well: She would have dollars in her fist. I would say I couldn't take money; my parents wouldn't approve. Then she would say it was just a little gift, and I would say no thank you.

It didn't go that way. Effie had a bad cold.

"Mark, you must not get near me. I don't want to make you sick. But come in, I have bread just from the oven."

Though her kitchen smelled like heaven, I didn't feel

122

very hungry. My stomach was too full of worry. I cut myself a small slice, because Effie didn't want to get near the loaf with her germs.

"Your mama tells me you have been writing letters. Are you getting good answers, I'm hoping?" Effie put the teakettle on the stove. "Are the army people going to send Volfie back to us next year?"

"I've heard back from our congressman, not from the senators yet. The congressman kind of promised to look into it. I haven't heard anything from the army."

Effie rinsed her blue-and-white china teapot at the sink. "It is good you are writing these letters. Wrong can get out of hand so quickly." She peered out the window. "I know this one thing, Mark: it does not take long." Effie accidentally hit the teapot against the faucet, and a chip of white flew off the spout.

Effie loved the few beautiful things she'd brought with her from Germany. I thought she'd be sad that she'd put a nick in her teapot. But she went on gazing out the window with the faucet still running, and didn't even notice.

* * *

I rode my bike to school and back almost every day now, even though we were getting one snowstorm after another. Some days I had to walk my bike most of the way because the snow was coming down so hard. But I couldn't stand waiting around after school for the bus to load, then the slow trip home while the bus dropped kids off. I wanted to get home fast so that I could check the mail.

At the end of the week, I had a letter. Not from the senators or the army, but from Wolfie. A short one.

Dear Mark,

    Taking off in morning. We been busy.

    My biskits got here, tell Effie thank you. I mean, Woof! HA! Tucker says thank your mom for cookies, paper, pens, and the grammar book. He is going to read the English book on the plane because it will be a long trip. I will be in a crate and I won't like that.

                 Love,

                 Wolfie

14

The letters I'd been expecting all came within a couple days of each other. I took them to school to show Mr. Casey.

Mr. Casey had put up new pictures of Washington, Jefferson, and Lincoln. And he had a new bulletin board—a map showing where the Underground Railroad had operated when it smuggled slaves out of the South.

Mr. Casey leaned back in his chair, long legs stretched in front of him, feet in worn-out shoes. He smiled at the return addresses on the envelopes I'd handed him. "One from each of the senators, one from the army. This is very, very good, Mark." He looked from envelope to envelope like they were Christmas packages and he couldn't decide which to open first.

I hoped he could find something encouraging in them. I felt pretty down.

He chose the one from Senator Corbett and unfolded it.

"'Dear Mark,'" he read aloud. He nodded as he read the next part to himself. He began to frown. "'Our office cares about your concerns and will do everything possible

125

to bring them to the attention of specialists in charge of the matter.'" He looked at me. "Sounds like a line they use to everyone who writes." He continued reading. When he got done, he turned the page over to look at the back, and checked in the envelope for more pages. "This is it?"

"What do you think?" I asked.

"I'm . . . disappointed. It's so vague. I was hoping they would promise to do something specific. But . . ." he lifted his brows ". . . two to go."

After he read the second letter, he refolded it, shaking his head. "I feel bad about this, Mark. I urged you to write and expected your letters would get these guys moving. Maybe if you were voting age . . ."

He picked up the one from the army. "At least *these* guys can't pass the buck."

He read aloud, "'Dear Mark, thank you for your letter and your interest in the army's Military Canine Program. Dogs have served in the U.S. Army dating back to the Civil War and have been valued as an asset to national defense because of their unique capabilities with regard to scent, sight, and hearing.'" Mr. Casey nodded impatiently. "'Dogs continue to serve with our fighting forces, distinguishing themselves for bravery, loyalty, and service beyond the call of duty.'" He blew air out his cheeks. "I hope this gets better.

"'Your letter was forwarded to me and I have taken note of your concern about what will happen to the war dogs after the Vietnam conflict is over. The army is considering several options and has not yet decided on a single plan. It may be that several different plans for disposing of the dogs will be implemented, based on considerations such as an individual dog's state of physical and mental health, length of service, and prospects for rehabilitation.'"

Mr. Casey got a terrible scowl. "What the hell does that mean!" Then he said, "Sorry." Teachers weren't supposed to cuss.

"That's okay." I liked that he was mad.

"I don't like the sound of 'disposing' of the dogs."

"Yeah."

"They must mean how the dogs will be dispersed, but I wish they'd said it differently. And what's this 'several options' garbage? If they don't know the plans for the dogs, who does?" He flicked the letter with his fingers. "You sent such a good, strong letter. That's all you got from them?"

"They sent me another eight-by-ten picture of a Huey, suitable for framing."

"Great."

Mr. Casey tapped his scuffed foot. "Mark, we can't get discouraged."

I was. "They didn't even mention Wolfie."

"I hoped for better. But remember, I said you might have to take it to a higher court?"

"Oh no."

Mr. Casey waited.

"Okay, what?"

"Start a petition."

"You don't mean standing at a shopping center and asking people to sign a paper?"

"Yes. You'd need a lot of help for that. To make it count, you'd need to station people at every shopping mall in the county some Saturday."

"I don't know that many people."

"You might have to call for help from sympathetic groups."

"You mean from groups who oppose the war?" Dad ought to really go for that.

Mr. Casey pulled up a student desk to sit in. It made a terrible scraping noise.

"I don't know," I said.

"It would mean a lot of work." He grinned. "It'd be worth a lot in extra credit. None of my students has ever undertaken such a thing."

I sat in silence.

"Or, you might want to put together a protest." His eyes kind of gleamed.

"Like the ones on TV?"

"Not that big, of course. You could stage a local protest, have someone take pictures of it, and send them to the army. The army knows it has a problem with the public; it might respond if it thought more people than you are upset."

"I don't know if a protest would be okay."

"It's more than okay! It's your constitutional right. The First Amendment says, 'Congress shall make no law respecting an establishment of religion, or prohibiting the free exercise thereof; or abridging the freedom of speech, or of the press; or the right of the people peaceably to assemble, and to petition the government for a redress of grievances.' You're covered, under peaceable assembly and free speech."

That's not what I meant. I was thinking about Dad, who wouldn't like a protest any more than he would a petition. Less, probably.

I sat in silence. Wolfie's face, with its fringe of uneven hairs, kept appearing in my mind.

Mr. Casey sucked on his bottom lip.

"So, in the U.S., if we don't agree with something, we can go out and march against it?"

"Absolutely."

"Why don't people march against paying taxes?"

"They do."

"People still pay them."

"It would take lots and lots of people marching. Most people agree that the government needs money to finance the military, build roads, oversee the national parks, and administer social security. That money comes from taxes. People generally don't protest taxes, they just complain about them. On the other hand, hundreds of thousands have shown up for causes like civil rights for blacks."

"I wouldn't be able to get even a hundred people."

"You wouldn't have to. The protests on behalf of blacks are intended to change a national policy. Your goal would be to just get the army's attention."

"How many people would need to show up?"

"I'd say if you had twenty to thirty, enough for a picture to send to the army, you could feel like it was successful."

"I wouldn't know where to start."

"Help is available."

* * *

When Dad came home, he turned on the TV. I stretched out on the floor to watch the news with him. A picture came on of an airstrip in Vietnam, with body bags holding dead soldiers lined up on the runway for shipment back to the U.S.

"Shut it off!" Dad said.

I went to my room, lay down on my bed, and stared

at the ceiling. The ceiling plaster had pictures in it. One looked like a guy on horseback, with the horse rearing up like it was going into battle.

* * *

Mom and I went Christmas shopping for what she and Effie called "our soldier boys"—Danny, Wolfie, and Tucker. Danny was used to spending Christmas vacation skiing with friends and tobogganing on the hill behind the fire station, and Mom wanted to be sure he'd have something to cheer him up in the hot jungle.

We found a poster with a scene of snowy mountains and pine trees loaded with snow. We also found a really cool knife that had a pearl handle, plus a smaller knife, can opener, nail clippers, and tweezers.

I said, "Doesn't the army issue stuff like that?"

"They sound like they're low on everything where he is. I'm going to guess he doesn't have anything this nice."

"Did you see the price?" I sounded like Dad.

"I'm spending my December checks on Christmas." Her chin went out.

"Okay. But don't forget how much it costs to ship things."

"We only have to get it to San Francisco. The army takes it the rest of the way."

I told myself to quit raining on Mom's parade.

A display of plastic ropes hung next to the knives. I picked one up and held the knife to it. "Don't ever sneak up on me like that again, Snake." I made the rope lunge at Mom. "Should we get a knife for Tucker, too?"

"I have something *so* good in mind for him." She hunched her shoulders like a kid with a secret.

"What?"

"After we finish here, we'll go to the bookstore."

At the bookstore, she picked up two books from the children's section, *Charlotte's Web* and *Where the Red Fern Grows.*

"These are for little kids."

"Don't you remember how much you loved them?"

"Yeah. I was in third grade."

"I talked this over with a high school reading teacher, and she said that if Tucker has trouble writing, he struggles with reading, too. She said to get him some excellent children's books."

"Isn't *Where the Red Fern Grows* too sad?"

"I thought about that. But a grown woman checked it out of the library one day and said she was going to read it because she needed a good cry." Mom twisted the strap on her purse. "Everybody does, sometimes."

I got to choose the gifts for Wolfie. I found a cool new Frisbee that was supposed to fly farther and a huge rawhide bone. Those presents were lightweight enough that Tucker wouldn't mind packing them. I also bought Wolfie a silver bell to wear on his collar.

Mom said, "I'm pretty sure they don't want people to hear him coming."

"He can wear it at camp. It has a happy sound."

"Okay."

At home, I wrapped the presents while Mom started sorting cookies into metal containers and putting cellophane on the nut breads. She had been baking every minute she wasn't at work, and the house smelled great.

I told Mom we had enough baked stuff for a regiment, and she said, "There is plenty to share." When we added Effie's cookies and Christmas breads to our own, it made an even more impressive pile.

Mom and I were trying to analyze how to pack things so that the cookies wouldn't break. Dad listened from his recliner for a few minutes, then put down his book and offered to help us. Mom thanked him about six times. I said thanks, too, because it was a relief to have him involved.

Getting the stuff off to Vietnam distracted me for a few evenings, but the rest of the time I felt gloomy. Christmas wouldn't be much fun without Danny and Wolfie. Christmas morning would be just the three of us, and Dad had been moody lately. Effie would come for dinner, and that part would feel normal. Maybe we could persuade Dad to play "White Christmas" on his trumpet.

I tried to catch up with my homework. Miss Thompson had agreed not to call my folks, and I had done two makeup assignments in her class. But it was hard to concentrate on algebra. I would get in the middle of figuring a problem, then find myself trying to figure out how to help Wolfie. I had my regular homework, too, and tended to fall asleep doing it. Not that it wasn't boring, but I wondered why I felt sleepy all the time.

One night Mom came in my room and moved my English book from under my head. I woke up.

"Maybe you ought to get ready for bed."

I nodded.

"Go do your teeth and then come back."

"Okay."

I stumbled back from the bathroom.

"It's only seven-thirty, but if you're sleepy, go ahead and go to bed," Mom said.

"Okay."

"How's everything going?"

I shrugged.

"Anything you want to talk about?"

"I'm thinking about putting together a protest."

She kept her face in neutral. "Protesting what?"

"What I talked about in the letters I sent."

"Don't schedule anything during the holidays—people are too busy. And January is cold. Plan it for February."

"Okay." In that short conversation, the protest changed in my mind from a pipe dream to something real.

The next day, I told Mr. Casey. He tried to look nonchalant, but couldn't pull it off; his face stayed expressionless, but his heels bounced up and down on the floor.

Now that I'd decided to stage a protest, all kinds of questions crowded my mind. Where would I hold it? Would we carry signs? What would the signs say? How would I get people to come?

One night when Dad was at a parent-teacher conference and Mom was in the bedroom folding clothes, I surprised myself. I got up from my bed, walked to the kitchen, picked up the phone, and dialed Claire's number.

She answered.

"Do you know how to put on a protest?"

"Is this Mark?"

"Yeah."

"My parents have helped with some."

"Would you help me put on a protest?"

"What are you protesting?"

"The army, because they don't know what they're going to do with Wolfie and the other dogs after the war."

"Count me in. You could come over to my house after school on Friday. Peggy knows a lot about protests."

"Who?"

133

"Peggy. My mom."

* * *

After school the next day, I went to the gym and watched Rick and the others doing basketball drills. Rick saw me in the bleachers and grinned and waved. When he aimed and shot, he sank it like it was nothing. Some of the other guys got real tense when they took aim, but Rick stayed loose whether he was shooting or dribbling or guarding. The other guys seemed to like him, too, even though he was a year younger, and smaller.

I waited for practice to end, to walk home with Rick. It was another cold day, and I shivered while I talked.

"So, when are you going to do this protest?"

"February."

"Will it be a lot of work?"

"Claire's going to help."

"Aaah." Rick looked at me from under his eyebrows. "So, this isn't really for Wolfie; it's an excuse to hang around a fine chick."

"I don't need an excuse. She's insanely in love with me."

"I overheard her say that, in just those words."

I punched his arm.

We reached his house. The white dry-cleaning van was parked in the driveway. Rick got a serious face, and this time it wasn't pretend. "Uh-oh."

"Why do say 'uh-oh' when your dad's home?"

Rick shrugged. "No reason, I guess."

I kept looking at him.

"You know dads."

"No." Dad had been hard to read lately, but I didn't say 'uh-oh' when I saw his car.

Rick put his easy smile back on. "Hey, thanks for waiting for me. I'll see ya tomorrow."

"I don't have to go yet."

Rick waved toward the house. "I gotta . . . ya know."

"You don't want me to come in."

He didn't deny it.

"Because of the protest? I won't say anything about it."

"No, man!"

"Let's stay out here and talk." I wanted to tell him about Mr. Casey, and the awful makeup assignment I was working on in Algebra, and what I'd bought to send Wolfie for Christmas.

"I oughta . . . Greg . . ."

"What?"

"Greg gets nervous."

"When your dad's home?"

"He's a fidgety kid."

I took Rick's coat sleeve. "What's up?"

He pulled his arm away. "Nothin'."

I looked at his house with the yellow shutters where I'd played as a little kid and where I hadn't visited much lately, and it hit me, like it should have before, that Rick kept me away whenever his dad was home. I started remembering times when I'd said I was coming over, and Rick would say he was coming to my house instead.

"You're not going." I grabbed hold of him again.

Rick looked away, frowning. He didn't try to throw off my hand, though, and after a minute said, "Dad drinks. And then gets mean."

"How come you never said anything?"

"I gotta go. Greg gets scared."

I let loose of him. Rick walked toward his house. When

he got to the edge of his yard, I said, "Wait a minute," and hurried and caught up with him. "After this mess with Wolfie gets solved, I . . ." I didn't know how to say it. "I want to take a turn. Being your friend."

Rick kept his head turned away. But he nodded.

15

"Maybe you should schedule the protest for the middle of the month." Claire said. "I'll go get a calendar."

She got up from her living room floor and maneuvered around a three-foot wall of books and magazines. I'd asked her, "What are these for?" and she'd said, "Research," but what I'd really meant was, what were they doing in the living room, taking up most of the floor?

Claire's mother, Peggy, sat on a big pillow, notebook in her lap, paging through a magazine. She wore a faded skirt, small round glasses, and bunny bedroom slippers, but even so, she moved in kind of a queenly way, like Claire. When Claire had introduced me to her, Peggy had looked into my eyes with so much curiosity, I'd had to look away. It had felt like a compliment.

Claire came back carrying a calendar and grinning. "Look! The Saturday in the middle of February is February fourteenth. Valentine's Day. Perfect."

"What does Valentine's Day have to do with a protest about dogs?" I asked.

Claire blinked. Her cheeks went red. Her lips made an O, but no word came out.

Her mom said, "Love and peace."

Claire said, "Yeah," and let out her breath. A look passed between Claire and her mom.

"You'll have to call the county to see about a permit." Claire pointed at my notebook. "Write that on your list. You'll need to buy supplies to make signs for people to carry. Where will you get the money?"

I shrugged.

"How will you publicize it?" Peggy asked.

I shrugged.

"Would you like some suggestions?"

"Sure."

"You can put up posters at places like schools, the record shops, and the library. If you have a budget, get the posters printed; otherwise, it will take you forever to make them by hand."

"Right," I said, even though I had no budget.

"You'll need to send a news release to the radio station and the newspapers. If they run it, that will give you wider publicity than you can get with posters."

I was floundering in the deep end, and I'd meant to stay in the wading pool. "I don't want a lot of publicity," I said.

Claire and Peggy looked at each other.

"How do you expect to get people to come?" Peggy asked.

I thought about it. There had to be another way.

Another look passed between Claire and Peggy, and they busted out laughing.

"We're not laughing at you, Mark," Peggy said.

"Yes we are," Claire said. "We are most definitely

laughing at you." Then they laughed some more.

"It's my night to make dinner," Claire said. "You can come in the kitchen if you want."

While Claire pulled things out of the cupboard and started mixing up muffins, she helped me finish the list of things I'd need to do. Peggy called from the living room that she'd help me put together a news release. She said Nathan, Claire's dad, might be willing to take pictures. Claire said she'd help me put up posters.

"What's your mom researching?" I asked Claire.

She frowned. "Researching? She's gone back to college, but she's not researching anything."

"All those books . . ."

"Oh. They belong to my little brother, Dirk."

"How old is he?"

"Ten."

"Those are all his?"

"Mm-huh."

"What's he researching?"

"Grasshoppers."

I nodded. Several times, actually.

"He's researching whether they could work as a food source. They're high in protein, and you know, there's a big supply of them."

"Sure."

Claire glanced at me. Then she started to laugh again, and her mom in the living room laughed, too.

I didn't mind. The afternoon had put me in a great mood. Claire had offered to go with me to put up posters.

* * *

The Christmas card Danny sent showed a night sky with lots of stars. Gold letters said JOY TO THE WORLD.

139

Danny had included two pictures, one of him alone, one with another soldier.

In the one where he was alone, Danny was leaning against a tree. He had a stubble of beard and no shirt. On the back he had written, "Danny, the Boonie Rat."

In the other picture, Danny and his buddy had draped ammo belts across their bare chests and around their waists. Danny had written on the back, "Fred and I, decorated for Christmas."

Mom held the picture close to her eyes. Next, she opened the card and read what was printed inside. "'In this season of peace, may you find great joy.'"

"Pretty card, and a nice message," Dad said.

Mom stared at him.

"What'd I say now?" Dad asked.

"*Bitter* card," Mom said. She sort of tossed the card and pictures onto the coffee table. "Who would have thought it? Our Danny, bitter."

I couldn't get my breath; the tension had sucked the air out of the room.

I picked up the card to see if Danny had written anything personal to us. He had. I read that out loud. "'I will miss you all during the holiday, wish I could be home. I've mailed your presents, hope you get them on time.

"'Say a prayer for me, if you think of it.'"

Dad said, "I've never known Danny to be religious."

Mom, sounding bitter herself, said, "He's scared."

* * *

Mr. Casey studied my list. "This is good, Mark. A lot of things on here that I hadn't thought about, like a budget. Is that going to be a problem?"

"I don't have much money."

"Maybe the money could come from a sympathetic group."

"I wouldn't want to take money from . . . I'm not really against the war."

"How about the Humane Society? Those are people who love dogs and would share some of the concerns you have."

On Saturday morning, I walked to the animal shelter where I used to visit before I got Wolfie. I had gone back once, when Wolfie was about a year old, to show them how he had turned out, and the volunteers had made a big fuss over him and told him he was beautiful.

Even though I hadn't been back since, one of the women recognized me and asked how my big dog was. So I told her where Wolfie was, how he got there, and how the army wouldn't say what plans they had for him after Vietnam. I told her it wasn't just Wolfie, either, and explained about the dog handler who was trying to bring his dog back with him. She listened like she was hypno-tized, and then called over a woman named Mrs. Bates and asked me to retell the story. I was glad to do it because this time I remembered to tell about the protest. Mrs. Bates listened hard, like the first woman had. I don't know if I would have had the courage to ask for money, even though Mr. Casey had told me a tactful way to say it: I was to say I was looking for sponsors. But I didn't even have to do that, because Mrs. Bates asked me if there was a way the Humane Society could get in on the action. "After all," she said, "Wolfie is one of ours." I said I needed money for printing publicity posters and making signs for protesters to carry, and walked out with a check for three hundred dollars. That was way more than I would have asked for, but when I called Claire to tell her the news, I got Peggy and she said, "It will take every penny of it."

* * *

I leaned against the gymnasium wall and watched the junior varsity basketball guys doing a passing drill. Finally, I spotted Rick at the other end of the gym, practicing three-point shots. He waved in his usual happy way.

I stayed until practice was over, and we started off for home together. Then he seemed different—not very glad to see me. For one thing, he walked so fast I could hardly keep up. Usually, Rick and I could be okay not talking, but this time he ran a quiz show, asking me one question after another about Claire, Wolfie, and Danny.

I caught on. The day in front of his house, Rick had rolled down the window a little on his family's private life. Now, the window had gone back up, and that's where he wanted it to stay.

* * *

The money from the Humane Society made the protest official in my mind. I wanted Dad to hear about it from me, rather than someone else, but I dreaded that conversation. Every time I had a chance to tell him, I gave myself an excuse not to: Dad looked tired, Dad looked grumpy, Dad had driven home on slick roads. Next morning, I'd promise myself that this would be the day, right when he got home, and I wouldn't chicken out again.

On Thursday, the day he taught orchestra, his favorite class, Dad came home in a jolly mood. An exchange student, a violin prodigy, had joined the class and would be

142

playing with Dad's orchestra for the next nine weeks. "I'll use him as a soloist at the next concert," Dad said. "What a privilege to work with someone so talented. Everyone in the orchestra tried harder today; this kid gives the others something to aspire to." Dad opened the refrigerator and got out a plate of vegetables and dip Mom had made. "Come have some cauliflower, Mark, it'll put hair on your chest." He rubbed the top of his head. "Maybe I ought to have some cauliflower."

I looked out the window. The sun gleamed on melting patches of snow.

"I'm going to be putting on a protest march," I said.

He bit a carrot stick in half. "Protesting school lunches or too much homework? Those are the two biggest complaints at my school." He stopped chewing, like he suddenly remembered my letters to the army. "Wolfie?"

"Yeah."

I almost regretted that I'd waited for a day when he was cheerful, because now I had to watch the good mood seep out of him.

"Maybe you need to trust that the army is taking care of things. You may want quick answers, but it can be more complicated than you understand. Sometimes, Mark, we have to trust our institutions. Some people don't want to do that these days, but if this country had fractured a dozen different ways during World War Two, we wouldn't have defeated Hitler."

I had expected this lecture. When I got a chance I said, "It's not that I'm against the war."

"Seems like you're against the army."

"I don't like how they're treating my dog," I said. A pain started behind my eyes.

I put some vegetables and dip on a plate and went to the

143

living room. I turned on the television, and the five o'clock news had started.

"Leave that on," Dad called from the kitchen.

Like always, there was footage from Vietnam. I searched the screen for a glimpse of Danny, Wolfie, or Tucker. So far, I hadn't seen a dog and handler on any clips. As for Danny, how would I know him? The soldiers all looked alike in helmets and identical clothes, running across the screen, or riding in jeeps, or firing guns.

Dad sat down in his recliner. The scene changed from Vietnam to New York, where a demonstration was going on. "Here we go," Dad said when the camera showed long-haired, angry-looking guys yelling at police. "The Great Unwashed at it again."

In this demonstration, a group of men carried signs that said, "Vietnam Veterans Against the War." Most of them looked like the hippies, with beards and long hair, but a few had short, military haircuts. One guy on crutches held up a medal for the cameramen.

"That's a Bronze Star," Dad said.

The guy with the medal dropped it into a box with other medals. The reporter said the veterans were mailing their medals back to Washington.

"Look at that! A Bronze Star and Silver Stars and Purple Hearts in that box." Dad shook his head.

"What did they get those medals for?"

"Purple Hearts go to people who were wounded in action," Dad said. "Bronze and Silver Stars are awarded for extreme bravery. And to think those guys don't want those medals!" Dad stared at the screen like he was watching an invasion by Martians. "I hope our boys serving over there don't see this."

We had potato salad and chicken for dinner, and Mom

144

noticed that I hardly touched it. After Dad went into the living room she said, "Aren't you feeling well?"

"Will Danny think I'm betraying him? I mean, with my protest?"

"Mark, you see his letters. Don't you see that he . . . ?" She glanced into the living room.

She wouldn't say any more, even though I bugged her.

16

I moved presents out of the way and sat down on the floor beside the Christmas tree. I held a thick envelope containing my first real letter from Wolfie since he'd been in Vietnam.

A couple of gifts under the tree—the ones from Claire and Danny—had me really curious. But the letter from Wolfie would be my top present. It had arrived in the nick of time that afternoon, Christmas Eve.

Mom knelt down and plugged in the tree lights. "Maybe you want to wait to read that until after tomorrow."

I looked at her like she'd just stepped off a spaceship.

"It usually takes me a day or so to recover from a letter from Danny."

"It does?" I hadn't known that. The way she called Effie right away, I thought it felt to her like winning the Irish Sweepstakes.

No way could I wait to hear how things were going for Wolfie and Tucker. I stretched out on the floor to read.

Dear Mark,

When we got to Japan and Tucker took me out of the crate, I couldn't hardly move. It was like I was kripled. Tucker said he couldn't hardly walk either. So him and me went out and walked around the air force base and in a few minutes I was okay and wanted to play, but Tucker was tired out still and didn't want to. He let me off the leash to have a good run. I seen a air force sentry dog while I was out running and wanted to go meet him but Tucker called me back because he said that dog would be one mean Jose.

We had flew over the North Pole at 40,000 feet. When we started to land in Japan, we saw mountains and rice paddies. It felt a long ways from where I used to live with you in Colorado, and Tucker said Kentucky seemed like a place he'd made up.

It took us six more hours to get to Vietnam after that. The first thing I seen in the runway lights when we started to land was some wrecked planes. By that I don't mean wrecked. I mean they had been bombed.

We got in at 11 at night and the temperature was 110 with 100 purcent humidity. Fort Benning had cooled off good the last couple months, so it was hard to take the change.

It took us forever to get processed. Sometimes I had to be in the crate, sometimes I could stand in line with Tucker. You should see how popular I am. Everybody was happy to meet me. Some soldiers coming in from the field was dirtier than pigs, but before they even went to wash up, a couple come over to see me. They asked Tucker if I was mean and if they could pet me. Tucker just laughed at that. He said, "He ain't near mean

147

enuf." One guy said, "There's enuf meanness over here, we don't need more."

The dirtier of the two guys stayed and petted me a long time. He told Tucker he would look out for me if Tucker wanted to go look around, but Tucker said no thanks. After they left, Tucker brushed me. He hated to have someone who stunk so bad hanging on me. He told a guy in line that he'd find a way to stay clean and the guy says, "Let's see what you say after you been in the bush for a couple weeks."

We had to be up early next day to be taken to our camp. A lot of guys was lined up waiting for buses or planes. Tucker kept pouring water in a pan for me, but he couldn't keep up with how thirsty I was. Guns and mortars was exploding in the distance, and it made the new guys nervous.

We didn't get out that first day, but the next day we got on a cargo plane and was flown to our new camp. It was back in the crate for me.

On the plane, we heard stories about the country and the weather. A guy told Tucker that it's always rainy except when it ain't. Then the ground gets hard like cement and the elephant grass falls over. When it starts raining again, it goes for weeks, and the elephant grass grows a few inches a day. Nobody has stood up yet to say they think it's a good climate here.

Reading the letter, I saw how Danny had been protecting Mom and Dad from worry. He didn't mention things like guns and mortars exploding within hearing distance.

Tucker's going to be two feet shorter when he gets home. He got ishued his gear and it's going to bust his

148

*back to carry it all. He got a rucksack, six canteens for
water, hand grenades, flares, ammo for his M16, LRP
and C rations, dog food, and vet tablets for me if I get
sick.*

*Tucker wonders if this will be as much of an adven-
ture as he thought. He still wants to chase Charlie out
of the jungle and run him back to North Vietnam, but
he don't like what he hears about the enemy. They are
small but dangerous. The air force base where we landed gets hit with rockets every night. The base is guarded
and has wire around it, and they send patrols out at
night to find Charlie, but they hardly ever do, and
instead they get ambushed.*

*We are in tents that hold rows of cots, but when we
go to the field, it will be damp ground for us. You can
see, we're homesick already and we just got here. I bet
when I lived with you I had a favorite rug to lay on. I'd
give a lot for that right now.*

*It don't seem like it's almost Christmas, except that
when we walked past a medic tent, we seen a nurse had
put a jungle plant in a pot and decorated it with ribbon.*

*Tell your Mom that Tucker is going through the
exercises in that book she sent. Maybe you notised his
spelling has got better.*

Merry Christmas from Tucker and me.

Wolfie

* * *

Mom had hot cinnamon rolls waiting when I got up
Christmas morning.

I stumbled into the kitchen feeling like a wreck. I
never slept much the night before Christmas, but this time
it wasn't from being spun-up and excited. What kept me

awake this time were pictures in my head of bombed-out planes on an airfield, Wolfie and soldiers crowding to get onto buses and planes, and patrols going out where ambushes waited.

Dad told Mom the cinnamon rolls smelled wonderful and put his arm around her shoulder. I didn't want to be a drag, so I said, "Merry Christmas, everybody."

"Looks like you made a haul, Mark. Want to open a present first or have some of those good rolls?"

I wanted to open Claire's present. But the way Dad was eyeing the rolls, I said, "Let's eat first." So we ate. I felt a little sick when I got done, but that's just how it was with my stomach these days.

Dad brought his hands together in a clap, rubbed his palms together, and said, "The first present goes to Mark, and I'm delivering it. Which will it be, Mark?"

I pointed to Claire's gift, a small box in silky red paper tied with silver ribbon.

As soon as I did, I saw my mistake. I should have kept that present in my room and opened it by myself. I hadn't mentioned to Dad the times I'd gone to Claire's after school, and I was pretty sure Mom hadn't either. The last time Dad had heard anything about Claire was when I told the story about her brother being a draft dodger.

"Somebody did a beautiful job wrapping this." Dad looked at the tag. "From Claire, to Mark." He cocked his head. "Who's . . ." The cheerfulness he'd been trying for that morning started to go out of him, and his face clouded. "Is that the girl who asked you to the dance?"

"Yeah."

"Looks like she's still after you." Dad gave me a look meant to dissect. What he wanted to know was whether I liked her.

I reached out my hand for the package. Dad handed it to me. His mouth kind of drooped.

An avalanche of anger rumbled in my belly. Why did the war have to ruin even Christmas? Wasn't our family paying enough, with Wolfie and Danny over there? I saw myself get up and fling the present at the tree, shattering ornaments and lights, and stalk to my room, where I couldn't be coaxed out for the rest of the day, where I would write Wolfie and Tucker a long, long letter and then finally get some sleep.

I only pictured that, of course, and didn't actually do it, because our family stayed away from dramatic scenes. It was our way to go on as natural as possible, even though the day couldn't be changed back now. Besides, I wouldn't have done that to Mom, who was trying to make Christmas normal.

I pulled off the ribbon and the wrapping and found a small green box, the kind that holds jewelry. The box sat in my palm. What jewelry could Claire be giving me?

It was a necklace. And that was wild, because that is exactly what I had bought for her. The one I'd bought had a gold chain and one cultured pearl, and Mom said I had really scored.

A round medallion on a silver chain lay on the box's green cardboard liner. I didn't dare look at Dad; he hated necklaces on guys. I brought the medallion close to look at it, half expecting it would have a peace symbol on it, but it had triangles and circles engraved in a design.

Mom said, "Very nice. See if there's anything on the back."

I turned it over, and saw engraved words. I had to switch the light on because we hadn't opened the drapes yet. I silently read the words, "Know Thyself." I handed the necklace to Mom. She read the words to herself and handed the necklace back to me, not to Dad.

I held it up and told Dad, "It says, 'Know Thyself.'"

"From the Greeks," Mom said.

"I know the origin, Eve." Dad lifted his eyebrows at me. "You'll look like a bona fide hippie in that."

I ran my finger over the engraved design on the front, turned the medallion over, and felt the words, like I was reading in braille, then hung the necklace around my neck. I wondered if this meant Claire really liked me.

"Whose turn now?" Mom said.

Mom tried on the wool sweater Dad and I had bought for her, and it just fit. We had found her a warm hat to match. Danny had sent her a beautiful blue-and-gray silk scarf that happened to match her new sweater. When she draped the scarf around her neck and tied it at the ends, I noticed her hands were shaking.

The other presents from Danny were great, too. He'd sent Dad a boat carved out of horn. It had tiny oars and a dragon's head carved on the bow. The box for me was long and thin. I shook it, but couldn't make a guess.

It turned out to be a stuffed cobra. I took it to my room and tried it on my dresser, but it was too big, so I found a place for it in the living room, beside the sofa. "The first on our block to have a cobra," Mom said.

We stood there, admiring the cobra in silence. If Danny had been there, he would have had us laughing with funny stories about snakes. I glanced sidelong at Mom and Dad, wondering if they were missing him like I was.

I got a blue parka from Mom and Dad. My old jacket didn't fit anymore, and the new one was a lot warmer and looked good, too. From Effie, I got a comb-and-brush set, about the last thing I would have asked for, but I liked the unusualness of gifts she gave me. Maybe boys in Germany went for things like comb-and-brush sets.

Rick and I had bought each other candy from the bulk bins at Safeway. We had agreed not to wrap it, so we just put our sacks under the tree. I opened mine and ate a malt ball.

The last gift I opened came from Mom. Well, the tag said "Mom and Dad," but the way Mom perched on the sofa's edge when I picked it up, I could tell she had shopped for it.

It was four hardbound books, with the titles stamped in gold: *The Hobbit*, by J. R. R. Tolkien and the Lord of the Rings trilogy.

"Wow," I said. We generally got paperback books because of our budget.

"I thought these would be books you'd read more than once." Mom reached out and smoothed the cover of one.

I'd heard of them, and had thought about checking them out sometime.

Mom leaned over the end of the sofa and gave me a look that made us alone in the room. Alone on the planet, really.

"I thought about this a long time—what book would be entertaining and also have meaning for you. These will take you off to a completely different world, and I think you need that right now. But what I like most is, this is the story of a small person who consents to do a large, difficult thing. He doesn't know, at first, how hard it will turn out to be."

"Cool," I said. I started on the first book that afternoon, and by the time Christmas break was over, had finished two.

17

Dear Mark,

Thank you for my dog treats and toys. Tucker says
to tell all of you thanks a lot for the Christmas stuff. He
was a popular guy when the boxes arrived. He thought
he was going to have to fight to hang on to the stuff, but
then he decided it wouldn't keep in this climate so he
might as well pass it around. He said to tell you the
bread with orange flavuring was his favorite.

Sounds like you hang around a lot with that girl.
Tucker says he would give a lot to have a girl he could
talk to about the stuff going on in his head. He is doing
a lot more thinking than he used to.

Too bad that things are tense between your mom
and dad. Tucker says he wouldn't know anything different. His dad was always fussing at his mom, or
mean and drunk. Sometimes his dad disapeered for a
month or two.

The green fireflies here are as big as Frisbees and at
night I make a game of trying to catch them. Tucker
says he doesn't know where I find the energy for it,

154

because we walk all day and it's hot as blazes. The other night I was determined to catch one of them blinkers. I kept leaping into the air, leaping and falling, then racing after a different one, leaping and falling. I had the guys in stitches. A couple of guys decided to get in on the action and tried to catch one for me. They ran around swatting at them with their hats. The villagers watched the guys like they was crazy.

A problem here is figuring out who is on your side and who ain't. The enemy and friends look the same. And the friends ain't always friendly. Some South Vietnamese like the North Vietnamese better than their own government, and sometimes South Vietnamese soldiers actually are infiltraturs from the north.

One night, our lootenant woke us up real quiet and told us we would be moving out in the morning. We asked, "Where to?" He wouldn't say, just put his finger to his lips. The guys packed up without making no noise. Tucker told me not to make a sound. When the first light come, we got on the road. The villagers come out and waved to us and hollered at us to be careful in Lang Bee End, or some name like that. You had to wonder—the soldiers didn't have no idea where they were headed, but the villagers all knew. Tucker said that don't seem too safe to him.

We stayed at that place for almost a week. I had my dog food, but the soldiers ate with the local people. That made them nervous because of how some people feel about the Americans. At mealtime, the guys would look at their bowls and whisper, "I hope this ain't poison." They had to go ahead and eat because they was so hungry. No one got sick, so it turned out okay.

Everybody has got pretty jumpy. We are in another

new area now, and nobody gets much rest. Even though a guard is on duty, most of the guys sleep light. Maybe some person we visited with earlier in the day will show up at night and try to slit a throat. Tucker sleeps the best because I am curled up next to him and he figures if somebody come around, I'd hear. A couple other guys—one named Hawk and one named Robbins (called the Bird Brothers)—try to sleep near me too, because they feel safer.

That's all for now.

Love,
Wolfie

18

February sun beaming through the blinds laid stripes across the kitchen table where Dad sat. He bent over a bowl of cereal. "Mornin'," he mumbled.

I looked around. "No pancakes?"

"Your mom went off someplace this morning, before I got up."

I nodded. Dad knew the protest was today, but I guess Mom hadn't mentioned to him that she and the women from the library were making signs for it.

The protest didn't start until ten, and it was eight-thirty. I wanted the morning to speed by, but at the same time, I wanted the clock to stop dead. What if the protest was a bust? What if someone threw something at the marchers and a fight broke out? What if someone got hurt? Worse, what if no one showed up? Maybe people had only pretended to be interested.

I poured myself a bowl of Cheerios and then began shoveling them in, though I had no appetite.

Dad looked up from his bowl and said in a hoarse voice, "I won't be coming today, Mark."

I nodded.

"If you want an explanation . . ."

I shook my head. "It's okay." I knew his reasons.

I picked up my bowl and drank the remaining milk. So much had been happening, I'd had no chance to talk to Effie, and that gave me another excuse to hurry.

Outside, it felt like April, not February. Even at that early hour, I didn't need a jacket. Blades of grass beside the driveway were trying to turn green.

I felt kind of bad that Dad would be left out of things. Effie, Mom, and I would be gone all morning, maybe most of the day.

When Effie opened her front door, her face tilted into a happy smile. "Mark." She clasped her hands. "It is good to see you. Come in."

"I can't stay." I followed her into the house anyway, drawn by delicious cooking smells. "I wanted to make sure you knew what time the march is. Ten o'clock at Lindsay Park."

"Yes, in the paper I saw. Also, the television has spoken of it." Her face started to change.

"You can walk over with me if you want." I grinned. "We'll make you a special sign with a German accent, 'Home Our Dogs Bring.'"

Effie's eyebrows knotted and she stared at a corner of the rug.

"I'm sorry. It was a joke. You speak wonderful English. Mom says you speak better than we do."

She fluttered her hand in front of her face. "I know is joke." Her shoulders slumped. "I won't be coming."

"Effie! It's for Wolfie."

"Ya. Ya." She folded her hands and squeezed them together so tight her fingers turned white.

158

I had never seen Effie like she looked then, like double gravity was pulling on her face.

"Mark. For you, I would come. For Volfie, I would march. For me, I cannot."

I nodded. "Okay."

"You would like to know why?"

Something told me to say no. But I nodded.

"I have make a promise to myself a long time ago. Never to join a mob."

"Mob? This isn't going to be a mob. This is a protest." I blinked. "You yourself said a person has to stand up for what he believes."

Her features melted into misery.

"A mob for my Valter came. One day, they are our neighbors—'Hi Effie, Hello Valter, nice day, ya?' The next day, into the bank they come and drag Valter away. My sister, she comes for me in the car, tells me, 'Get in,' and off we drive. I must see Valter, I tell her, but she says, 'It is too late, he is off to prison.' From prison, he went to the camps. I never see again."

I played with the hem of my shirt.

"People in a group do not think. They become a pack of wolves!"

She looked at me.

"You, Mark, are young. You have much feeling. You march for Volfie. Your muzzer," she tapped her head, "always is thinking and could not be swept up in mob. But some who walk today care nothing for dogs."

"Then why would they come?"

Her mouth pulled into a frown "Bored." She blew air out her cheeks. "They nothing in life have, so they pick up sign, yes? They are part of cause, yes? And off they go." Effie picked up a flower vase and marched a couple of

159

steps. "Now, I am not so bored! Now, I have power! Now I drag the good husband from the bank or lynch the poor Negro with the rope."

When Effie set the vase down, it clanked against the glass coffee table.

I stood rigid as a rock, my heart thumping in my ears. I mumbled, "I gotta go."

I dashed across Effie's yard. When I got to my own, I slowed down. I shouldn't have bolted my Cheerios, especially on a jittery stomach. A sour feeling and a cramp had started in my gut. I didn't want to go through the kitchen where Dad sat, glum and disapproving, but I needed to get to the bathroom.

I took a breath and tried the birthday party trick I'd learned when I was six, tightening my chest and stomach muscles and shrinking my throat so nothing could wash up into it. But a minute later, I had to lean over the bushes and toss up my Cheerios and milk.

There was nothing else to come up. But I stood there a long time, leaning against the cold bricks of the house, gasping.

* * *

I walked my bike into the park's bike rack without looking across the street to the fountain area where people were to meet. "If only twenty people come," I told myself, "it will be okay."

The taste of mouthwash tingled at the back of my mouth, and my stomach still felt jumpy. I forced myself to look across the brown grass to the pool and fountain, which had been emptied for winter and wouldn't be refilled until summer. I blinked. Though it was only 9:10, thirty or so people were milling near the fountain. Mom and a couple of women had set up a long folding table, and beside it sat the boxes containing signs.

A bus, the big charter kind, pulled up just then. I thought it would turn around in the parking area and leave, but instead, it stopped. The doors opened, the sound of rock music floated out, and a bunch of people, mostly kids about Danny's age, began to jump out.

". . . thirty-five, thirty-six, thirty-seven . . ." I counted as each a person stepped out. "Forty-four, forty-five . . ." I counted fifty.

The kids moved to the lawn, laughing and yelling. One of the guys set a portable radio on top of a picnic table and turned the volume up. Some of the group started to dance.

I ran across the grass to the folding table. Mom saw me coming and came to meet me. She pulled her fingers out of her ears and yelled, "From Denver University."

"For *our* march?" I asked.

She nodded, grinning.

A man as skinny as a tree walked up to the folding table and spoke to one of the library women. The woman at the table pointed at Mom and me, and the man walked over to us.

"You're Mark," he said. The man's arm shot out and I started to shake his hand, but he grabbed me around the neck and gave me a strangling hug. Then he moved to Mom and embraced her the same way. Mom's eyes got wide and she tried not to be too obvious about wriggling free.

"I am Brother Rudy," the man said. His voice carried over the noise. Rumpled slacks and a long-sleeved silky shirt hung on his bony frame.

"Eve Cantrell," Mom said. "Are all of you from Denver University?"

"We represent several pacifist groups, most of which

161

have a connection to the University." He looked at me with a grave face. "We stand in solidarity with you today, Mark. It is wrong for humans to drag other species into our conflicts. Some people who came with us oppose only this war, some oppose violence and all wars. One girl on the bus said she's never joined any protest before—she is here simply because she loves dogs." He smiled, which didn't make his face one bit less solemn.

"Now, tell us your rules," he said.

Mom and I looked at each other. "Rules?"

"It's your march, and we want to conform to your rules."

I glanced at Mom and took a stab. "No littering?"

He nodded. "I'll pass that along. What else?"

It was hard for Mom to yell above the noise, so she pointed at the music, held her ears, and shook her head. Brother Rudy nodded.

"I'll ask them to turn it down. How about we let them get rid of some of their energy, then when the march starts, shut the music off altogether? Older participants shouldn't have to endure it. I consider myself in that number." He smiled in his sad-faced way.

"I assume you will lead the march?" he said to me.

I nodded. I hadn't thought about that detail, but I did know the route.

"We have signs and banners," Mom said.

"So do we," Brother Rudy said. "But it's your show, and we will use your signs or a combination of yours and ours."

"We prefer you use only ours," Mom said firmly, like the matter had been decided before now.

"What about the police?" Brother Rudy said.

"We have a permit; no problem there," I said.

Brother Rudy looked at me with his saddest smile yet.

"Sometimes that makes no difference. If they want to arrest someone . . ."

Mom and I looked at each other, alarmed.

"Many of us are trained in peaceful resistance. We do nothing to retaliate, but we make it as much trouble for the police as we can." This time when he smiled, his face got kind of happy.

Mom and I traded another look.

"We don't offer them our hands to handcuff and let ourselves be quietly led away. We make them carry us off." He patted Mom on the forearm. "We'll go through how this works for anyone who is interested about twenty minutes before the march starts."

He hugged us ferociously like before, and walked back to the bus. Mom looked at me and shrugged.

Jailing protesters would bring more publicity our way and that might be good for Wolfie, but the talk about arrests and police made me nervous.

I looked back at the group who weren't with the college kids. They were keeping their distance from the loud music. I recognized a few people from the neighborhood, though most were strangers. There were a couple of real old people, some kids my age, older teens, and several couples with little kids. Agate was there with Orion, and she waved like crazy and gave me the peace sign.

I felt like everyone was watching me, and I didn't know quite what to do next. I didn't have to decide, because just then two police cars drove up. I froze. The group standing far from the loud music stared at the cars, but the kids on the grass kept dancing, and several of them waved at the cops. One cop got out of his car and went over to talk to the other one. They didn't seem very interested in the protesters. After a minute I remembered that the police had always planned to be there, but the damage to my composure had already been done.

In the next half hour, the crowd swelled. I kept trying to count how many were there, but got confused by new people showing up all the time. My method was to start near the fountain and move clockwise. The last time I did it, I counted two hundred. After that, I lost interest in how many had showed up, because someone tapped me on the shoulder and when I turned around, Claire was standing next to me.

"You're here!" I said

"I told you I would be." Her perfect teeth gleamed. "What a great turnout. What do you want me to do?" Before I could answer, she said, "It looks like they need help handing out signs. Where did all these people come from? Do you have enough signs?"

"It doesn't look like they've gone through all the boxes yet. Hey, there's your folks." I waved at Nathan, who had his fingers in his ears, and Peggy, who had moved behind the tables to help Mom.

"They have enough help with the signs." I screwed up my courage. "I'd like you to stay here. With me." My voice went high on the words *with me.*

Claire didn't seem to notice. She gave me about the nicest smile I'd ever seen from her, and that's saying something. Even better, she moved close and took hold of my hand.

The tight, awful feeling in my body started to relax. But in its place, I started feeling light-headed.

"Let's walk around and see who we know," she said.

In a minute, she was waving and pointing out people from school. "Yuck, Dorweiller," she said when Gene waved at us. He was trying to balance a sign on his palm,

164

and a couple of girls were laughing their heads off. You could tell he'd already dropped the sign a lot because it was hanging funny.

Mr. Casey, long legs striding, came across the lawn.

"Congratulations, Mark. You've pulled a good crowd here. Hi, Claire. Did you help?"

She nodded.

"I better go get a sign." He looked over the lawn full of people and smiled. "It's great isn't it? Our right to protest." He strode off.

Claire stared after Mr. Casey like he was John Lennon. "He is sooo cool," she sighed.

Claire asked me a lot of questions then that I didn't have answers for. Would we start right at ten, or give people a few minutes to be late? Would we tell people where we wanted them, or would we let them line up on their own?

Brother Rudy, holding a megaphone, climbed on top of a picnic table.

"Who's that?" Claire asked.

"His name is Brother Rudy."

"Is he a Catholic brother?"

I shrugged. "What's that?"

"It's like a priest, only different. They live in monasteries."

"Are they religious?"

Claire gave me a look. "Um, they live in monasteries."

"They're allowed to . . . ?" I still wasn't used to the idea that people who joined protests weren't all hippies.

Brother Rudy called for everyone's attention. A guy reached over and flicked off the radio.

"How are we this morning?" Brother Rudy called in a big, expressionless voice.

The crowd clapped and hooted.

"We've come here today to help Mark Cantrell." He pointed at me, and everyone cheered.

"Wave!" Claire ordered.

"And dogs." Everybody cheered louder.

"I know Mark wants this to be a peaceful demonstration, as do we, so let's talk about how we might achieve that. But first, let's center ourselves. We come from various spiritual traditions, or no tradition at all, but I think we can all be comfortable with a moment of reverent silence." Brother Rudy bowed his head and closed his eyes. So did most everyone else, but some in the college group tilted back their heads and raised their arms and swayed.

I glanced over at Claire. She had her chin on her chest and her eyes squeezed shut. Her nose was almost perfect.

Brother Rudy looked up after a couple of minutes and opened his mouth to speak, but just then someone in the college group started to sing "We Shall Overcome." The others took it up instantly, and began to hold hands. Claire and I already were holding hands, and she started to sing, but I was too nervous.

The people from the neighborhood had moved in closer when Brother Rudy began to speak. They started to sing, too. One guy about Dad's age had a mighty voice, the kind that gives you chills, and was booming, "Deep in my heart, I do believe, we shall overcome—some day." Even Dad would have had to appreciate the guy's great singing.

After the singing, Brother Rudy asked, "How do we who believe in peace answer insults or even threats?"

A girl near the front in a flowered skirt yelled, "When I marched in Boulder two weeks ago with Students for a Democratic Society, someone spit on me." She had to scream to be heard. "I said to him, 'Peace, brother,' and handed him a flower." The college group cheered.

Claire shook her head. "My dad must be dying."

"Why?"

"He can't stand self-righteous peaceniks."

"Oh." I didn't understand at all.

Brother Rudy talked about how to get arrested the right way, by lying down and folding your arms across your chest, making yourself into a stiff board. It was important not to get into debates with anyone along the route, he said, and to turn the other cheek if anyone from the other side threw anything or insulted you.

I told Claire that Mom had wanted the college kids to use our signs, so she must have some worries about keeping control of the march.

"Let's line them up then, too," Claire said, "so we'll seem to be in charge."

And that's what she did. She went up and told Brother Rudy that the protesters should line up in this order: kids and faculty from Foothills Junior High School first, then the library employees, then the neighborhood supporters, then the big Denver University group who came on the bus. Brother Rudy made the announcement.

For the next few minutes, Mom, Claire, Nathan, and Peggy kept repeating that order, even though people insisted on milling around and acting lost. People came up to tell me they thought the march was a good thing, or told why they were against the war and when they turned against it. Some told me about their love for dogs and what their dogs were named. I didn't make very intelligent replies because my head was fuzzy and the whole scene seemed out of a movie or a dream or someone else's life.

Then, finally, everyone was lined up. Long banners that

167

took three people to carry were lettered with the words, BRING OUR FOUR-LEGGED HEROES HOME. Some marchers held signs mounted on sticks; others held up big poster board signs that said, WE CARE ABOUT OUR FOUR-LEGGED SOLDIERS, DOGS ARE NOT EQUIPMENT, and BRING BACK WOLFIE AND HIS FRIENDS. When a guy in bright pants and no shirt lifted a sign that said, THE U.S. MILITARY KILLS BABIES, Mom and Nathan moved over to him in a flash. Brother Rudy came over and put his arm around the guy and talked with him. Peggy handed the guy a sign that said, BE KIND TO MAN'S BEST FRIEND, and he took it.

Signs bounced in the air; the sun gleamed down on the park. Claire handed me a sign. "They made this one just for you." It said, DON'T TREAT WOLFIE LIKE A DOG.

"Let's go," Claire said to me, and pulled me with her to the front of the line, where Mr. Casey and Miss Thompson stood talking with kids. Claire stared at them. Her eyes got huge. "Mark," she whispered, "they're holding hands. Mr. Casey and Miss Thompson!"

Mr. Casey made a sweeping motion and said, "Here you go, Mark; take your place."

The policemen got into their cars. Claire pulled a whistle from her jeans pocket. "Shall I give the signal?"

"Sure," I said.

She lifted the whistle to her lips. I waited for her to blow it, but she didn't. It hung in her half-open mouth.

I looked to see what had stopped her.

An ugly van had pulled into the parking lot, and passengers were getting out. It took them a minute to unload, and when people saw who they were, silence fell over everything.

19

There were only nine of them, but they equaled more than all the rest of us. They looked just like pictures I'd seen in the newspaper and on television—long hair, scruffy beards, bandannas tied around their heads.

They were dressed in olive drab shirts and pants and combat boots, except for three guys who wore camo pants. You couldn't see what kind of pants the guy in the wheelchair had on because a blanket covered his lap.

"Vietnam Veterans Against the War." Claire said each word slowly. Then she turned to me. "It's not your march anymore."

I nodded.

The orderly lineup Mom and the others had brought about started to melt as people moved around for a better look. The park had grown quiet as a church, and even the college kids stood motionless. Little kids tugged on their parents, wanting to be lifted up to see what everyone was staring at.

One guy's shirtsleeve was pinned shut where his arm used to be; another had a black eye patch. Two guys, a burly white guy who walked like a bulldog, and a tall slim black guy, came straight toward me. The rest followed slower, keeping pace with the guy in the wheelchair.

"I'm Lou Townsend," the white guy said.

"I'm Andy Pierce," the black guy said. "You Mark?"

I nodded.

"A dog named Bull saved my life," he said. "He alerted us to an ambush. We would have been wiped out, ten or more of us, if the dog hadn't been there. Bull took a bullet and didn't recover."

I was too astonished by them showing up to say anything; I only stared.

"Okay if we march with you today?"

"Sure." I noticed that Andy had a Purple Heart and a couple of other medals pinned to his shirt. Lou had a Bronze Star.

"We march at the front," Andy said.

I nodded.

"We have our own signs."

Claire and I traded a quick look, then I nodded.

"So, we'll just slip up here, then."

Mr. Casey, in the meantime, had moved to the new arrivals and was shaking hands and telling them welcome. Mr. Casey was a lot more friendly to them than they were to him.

"Liggett," Lou called to the man in the wheelchair. "Take your place."

When the man wheeled past me, I saw he had no legs.

"You need any help?" I asked.

He glared at me.

"I could push, if you wanted."

He didn't answer, and wheeled himself to the front of the line.

170

The guy with the eye patch carried an armload of signs and got busy distributing them to the vets. The signs all said the same thing. END THE WAR IN VIETNAM. BRING BACK OUR SOLDIERS. Lou and Andy unfolded a banner that read, VIETNAM VETERANS AGAINST THE WAR, and took their places behind Liggett in the wheelchair.

Once again, we were ready. Claire looked at me. "Should I blow the whistle, or let them start?"

"They seem to know what to do."

Mom showed up just then, looking shaken, and, like Mr. Casey, went from veteran to veteran shaking hands and telling them it was an honor to have them. But the vets showed a different side to her—they acted a lot more polite.

Mom said something to the guy in the eye patch, and he took her elbow and brought her over to Lou and Andy.

"She has a son in Vietnam," he said.

Andy and Lou put down their banner, and each shook hands with Mom. Liggett leaned his head back over his wheelchair and looked at Mom.

"We like to have mothers of soldiers march with us," Andy said. "Are there any other mothers here who are against the war?"

I didn't know if Mom thought of herself as being against the war. She was just open-minded and had been expressing doubts about it. But with no hesitation she answered, "I'll find out." A minute later my soft-spoken mother was moving among the protesters, hands cupped to her mouth, yelling, "Are there any mothers of soldiers here?"

She came back with four other women. One I recognized as a librarian.

"Mothers go right behind Liggett," Lou said.

171

A couple of veterans surrendered their signs to the women. Liggett looked up at Mom and said, "Would you push me?"

"I'd be honored," she said.

So my mom, pushing a Vietnam veteran, ended up leading the march. Dad would have choked if he'd seen her. I made a fierce, silent wish that he wouldn't get curious and stroll over to see how things were going.

Liggett looked over at the cops, made a circular motion above his head, and the policeman in front turned on his car's flashing light. He pulled his car in front of Liggett, and off we went.

I'd been so surprised by the turnout for the march, I'd had no time to think about what to expect in the way of spectators. Maybe people would be lined up three deep, like they did for the July Fourth parade.

When we turned off Skyview Drive onto Seventh Street, I saw a fair number of people on the sidewalk or leaning against fences or streetlights waiting for us, but it wasn't close to being crowded. Many people had dogs on leashes at their sides, or little mop dogs in their arms.

As we started to draw near the first bunch of people, I saw them smile and get ready to applaud. But when they saw the veterans leading the march, they fell silent. While we passed by, not a single person said a word or clapped or made any noise at all. Many of the spectators looked at the sidewalk or into the distance as the vets walked by.

The vets themselves marched in silence.

After the vets passed, the onlookers started reading the signs we carried, and by the time the other marchers and the college kids passed, clapping started. The college kids responded to that, lifted their signs higher, gave the peace sign, whooped, and shouted, "Bring the dogs home!"

172

Dorweiller was a few feet behind me, making stupid comments, carrying his sign sideways, or tucking it in the back of his jeans so it rested against the back of his head. Mr. Casey waved at the spectators with his free hand, and beamed like a movie star. I glanced at Claire. She was so serious her face was like marble.

It went like that all along Seventh Street. Spectators were silent as owls when the vets passed; began to respond as my school passed; clapped by the time the library women, neighbors, and other marchers with their signs went by; and hooted and cheered for the college kids.

Claire said, "I think all the action is happening at the rear of this parade."

A vet whose bandanna had fallen down around his ear turned around and growled, "It ruins the fun when we show up."

Claire looked embarrassed and started to respond, but the guy had already faced forward.

Mom wheeled Liggett's chair into the intersection and turned onto Francis Boulevard. On this wider street, more people had congregated along the sidewalks. One man, maybe a newspaper photographer, had crawled up a ladder and was pointing his camera at us. At the next intersection, a television crew had set up.

My stomach, which hadn't been normal all day, tightened into a steel knot when I saw five pudgy men in triangular Veterans of Foreign Wars hats waiting for us, a half block away. They carried signs that said, SOLDIERS STAY UNTIL THE JOB IS DONE, and DOGS AND PATRIOTS DEFEND AMERICA.

The VFW group saw the Vietnam veterans. One of them, a large old guy, yelled, "You're a bunch o' crybabies!"

As the Vietnam veterans came near the VFW group,

a VFW man whose gray hair stuck out sideways from his hat rasped, "Damn ya! You're losin' the war. America never lost a war before you guys!"

The Vietnam vets looked straight ahead. The eye patch guy in front of me stumbled, but caught himself.

Claire turned and stared at the old man, then took hold of my arm. "What a terrible, terrible thing to say to someone who has lost an arm or an eye or his legs."

I meant to take her hand because she looked so sad, but I couldn't take my eyes off Mom. Her grip had tightened on Liggett's wheelchair until her hands looked like claws, and she walked with a flat, stiff step. I could only see the back of her head, but I knew she was pale with fury.

Effie had said that people didn't always know their real motives for coming to a protest. I think Mom was in that category, though that would have surprised Effie. Mom thought she had come for Wolfie and me, but now I saw that she was marching for Danny. And this time, I didn't feel jealous. In fact, I felt proud.

On Francis Boulevard, the spectators could see us from a long way off and started to cheer, but like before, when they saw the veterans, a hush came over them. After the veterans passed, the spectators relaxed and responded by clapping when they read the signs about the dogs.

We passed three groups of war supporters besides the VFW group, with only a handful of people in each group. They held signs backing the war, but they didn't say anything to us. Because we were speaking up for dogs, not many counterprotesters had come out.

We were nearing the end of the march when a group bunched on the right side of the street caught the attention of all of us, even the Vietnam veterans. A group of pug owners sat in lawn chairs and on blankets, cradling funny-looking little dogs with flattened noses. As we got close, the group held the dogs up. The dogs wore little jackets made of towels, with words, peace symbols, and flowers painted on the sides.

The slogans on the makeshift dog coats were hard to make out because the dogs were so small, so the crowd spilled over to the right to read the words. SUPPORT MAN'S BEST FRIEND, THE ARMY TREATS 4-LEGGED SOLDIERS LIKE DOGS, and SIC 'EM WOLFIE. As the marchers read the jackets, they applauded. The owners offered up the dogs for petting. Even the Vietnam vets fell for those little dogs with their scrunched-up faces and decorated jackets, and stopped to pet them or asked to hold them.

So the march ended on a happy note for most people. For our family, it was different.

Claire touched me on the arm while I was petting one of the pugs.

"Mark." She pointed.

In the middle of the street, hands in his pockets, a stunned look on his face, stood Dad.

Mom had spotted him already. She stopped, and turned the wheelchair slightly toward him. Mom and Dad looked at each other across that wide street, and then Mom, head up, pushed Liggett into the vacant lot where the march would end.

20

I started to open the front door, but stopped when I heard Mom and Dad arguing.

It was Sunday, the day after the march. I'd been at Claire's doing American History. I wanted to turn around and go back to her house.

Dad was saying, "He signed up because he wanted to."

"You've pushed the military since the boys were little." Mom's voice wasn't loud, but it pierced through the door.

"It's a way for them to go to college."

"That's only part of it."

A silence followed. I thought they'd become aware that I was on the porch. But after a minute Mom said, "It's a way for you to expand your own army career."

"What? I served my country."

"But you stayed in the States and played in a band. You missed the big war. You weren't part of the action. You regret that you don't have war stories like your friends."

"They needed people in the bands! You think I'd send

our sons to the army just so I could have stories to tell?"

"You rush over to Sevorn's A&P the minute a letter from Danny comes."

I squeezed my eyes shut. *Mom!* If they kept going like this, it would be hard for them to make up. I started to leave the porch, but then I heard my name.

"You won't have your 'the military is a good way to go to college' argument with Mark."

"What do you mean?"

"He'll have a college fund, because I've started it."

"That's why you went to work?"

"Yes!" Mom hollered that one.

I walked down the sidewalk slowly, hoping Effie would look out her curtain and invite me in. I wouldn't have ratted out Mom and Dad and told her they were fighting, but I would have liked to sit in Effie's good-smelling kitchen and drink tea from a beautiful cup.

* * *

A kid named Mark staged a protest,
Played a part in the nation's unrest.
Said, "I must have my dog back,
'Cause life has a big lack—
Of my friends, ole Wolfie is best."

I slipped the notebook off the top of my desk when Miss Thompson looked my way, opened my algebra book, and pretended to be absorbed in it. When I glanced across the aisle, Mimi Shepherd, one of the eighth-grade cheer-leaders, flashed me a smile.

After all the publicity about Wolfie, popular girls had started coming around. Those girls had never glanced my way before the newspaper and TV stories. Besides, football and basketball were finished, so they didn't have anyone to fall all over.

Belinda Smith, a dingbat girl with curly hair, started popping up at my locker, the bus stop, and in the cafeteria. One day she worked her way over to me and whispered, "Mark, I saw you on television. That was so cool."

"Uh-huh."

"If there is anything I can do to help you get your dog back, let me know."

"I don't think so."

Like she couldn't understand English, she said, "I'll expect to hear from you then."

Nothing changed in how Claire acted toward me. She scolded me when I didn't take part in discussions in American History, argued with me about whether the United States should be in Vietnam, and nagged me to do my Algebra. She told me to keep up the letter writing for Wolfie, or the protest would be for nothing.

"Mark," she'd say with a frown, "Wolfie can't speak for himself."

It wasn't all scolding. One day as we were walking down the hall, she all of a sudden took my hand and held it to her cheek. I dreamed about that through all my classes.

The Sunday after the march for Wolfie, the *Rocky Mountain News* had carried a story and picture. The reporter had told about how I donated Wolfie through the Canine Recruitment Program. The reporter hadn't talked with me during the march; he had gotten his information from other people, but his facts were right. Mom had groaned when she read one part of it, though. A girl from Denver University had told the reporter it wasn't only wrong to use dogs for warfare, but also that people shouldn't make them do tricks like sitting up and walk-

178

ing on their hind legs, or pulling sleds in Alaska, because the dogs didn't have any choice in the matter.

A TV station had run a story that weekend, too. They showed a picture of Wolfie and me that I'd loaned them, but most of their footage centered on the Vietnam Veterans Against the War.

The biggest thing that happened was when Dave Hartwell, a national radio commentator, picked up the story. For days, people called the house to tell us that they, or someone they knew, had heard it. One of Mom's library friends called the producers in Los Angeles and asked for a tape of the program. When it came, Mom, Dad, and I listened to it.

The story, in Hartwell's dramatic voice, started like this:

"Mark Cantrell, a thirteen-year-old Colorado boy, wanted to do something to help his country. His older brother, Danny, who is serving in Vietnam, had told him of the need for canine scouts to help our troops. Mark stepped up to the plate, sacrificing his best friend and constant companion, Wolfie, a lovable German shepherd mix.

"But Mark became worried when the army refused to tell him whether Wolfie would be returned to him after the fighting is over. So Mark enlisted the help of his history teacher, classmates, and fellow dog lovers, to put together a demonstration that . . ."

At the end, Dave Hartwell took a swipe at the military. He said citizens, particularly young people, ought to be able to trust the people whose duty it was to protect them.

When it was over, Mom smiled and said, "He embroidered it nicely for human interest and drama."

Dad said, "Dave Hartwell used to criticize opponents of the war, but lately he makes cracks about the U.S. Says

179

we think we're the policeman for the world. He's gone over to the traitors."

Mom winced at the word *traitor* and got up to do dishes. I wanted to follow her so that she wouldn't be alone in the kitchen, but worried it would look like I was siding with her.

That's how it was most of the time—walking a tight-rope to stay cool with both of them. Ever since the march, the tension between them had become worse. Once when I got up in the night to get a glass of milk, I saw Dad sleeping on the couch.

Dad and I were putting a salad together one evening, to go with the meatloaf Mom had made before she went to work, and my knife slipped and cut my index finger. Dad got me a bandage, and while putting it on me said with a false chuckle, "When your Mom went to work, we didn't know we'd be pulling KP, did we?"

"It's not much trouble to make a salad," I said.

"Your mother's job has ruined our family life. We eat so late, we hardly have any evening left. I sit down to watch a program and fall asleep ten minutes into it."

Dad had always done that, but I didn't say so.

Dad leaned over my hand to check the bandage. He put his face close to mine. In a low voice he said, "I'm not criticizing your mom. But that library job has given her funny ideas. She used to have her priorities straight. I blame the library that she has gotten such squirrelly notions these days."

I started chopping carrots again.

"She doesn't think things through. She embraces the ideas of the women she works with. These days, she disrespects my ideas."

"If she doesn't agree with you, it doesn't mean she disrespects your ideas."

Dad looked at me. The corners of his mouth sank. I'd finished the carrots, so I reached up and flipped on the radio. I turned it to the classical music station.

* * *

I had started riding my bike to school on warm days, so I dropped by Mr. Casey's room after school often.

The girls who were in love with him, and that was ninety percent of those who had him for a teacher, didn't realize he was a little strange. Once I caught him reading poetry out loud. He acted embarrassed and slammed the book shut.

"Do you like e. e. cummings?" he asked.

I shrugged.

"What poets have you read?"

"We read some Coleridge and Wordsworth in English."

"Oh, right, I heard Mrs. Steadman talking about that. I know you write limericks. Do you write other poetry?"

"No."

"You should." He tucked the book in his drawer and asked what I had heard from either Tucker or the army. I hadn't heard anything new from the army.

Another time when I walked into the room, he was circling his desk with a book in his hand. "Madison, Madison, Madison. What were you thinking of, man?"

I backed out silently and came back only after making a lot of noise in the hall. It was too embarrassing to catch him talking to a dead president.

Often, he asked me questions I had no answers for

at the time. But pedaling home or before going to sleep at night, I would figure out what I might have said.

"If Wolfie comes home after a year, how will you celebrate?"

"I don't know," I said. But while passing the park on my way home, I decided what I would do when Wolfie returned. I would take him to the park and throw balls for him as long as he wanted. I'd never done that, because my arm wore out before Wolfie did.

"If you can't win with the U.S. Army," he asked another time, "where will you take your cause next?"

I shrugged. But lying in my bed that night with the lights out, I remembered that Mr. Casey said elected officials had to be sensitive to voters. If I couldn't get results from my congressman because I was a kid, I'd persuade some adults to start writing letters. I might even get other congressmen besides my own interested.

At first, I went to see Mr. Casey one afternoon a week, but it kept increasing until I was going nearly every day. I liked talking to an adult about Vietnam, because I stayed away from the subject at home.

"When did you turn against the war?" I asked him.

"I had doubts from the start," he said.

"Don't we have to stop evil?" I asked. "What if no one had stood up to Hitler?"

"You think this is similar?"

"I don't know."

He gazed at me.

"Well, yeah, I do." But actually, I didn't know what to think. Claire had told me that the North Vietnamese people saw their leader, Ho Chi Minh, as an Abraham Lincoln. Claire said that Ho had gotten his ideas about self-government from studying the U.S. Constitution and

182

Declaration of Independence. The Vietnamese people had gotten tired of foreign countries trying to rule them. Claire said the United States thought it knew what was best for other countries, but it didn't.

* * *

A letter arrived from Wolfie.

Hi Mark,

I kept my ears up the whole time Tucker read me the letter about the march you put on for me. Tucker hasn't liked the protests back home. He says if spoiled college kids had to work for a living, they wouldn't have time to be demunstrating. But a march for us dogs is a good thing, in his opinyun.

Tucker read your letter to everyone, and everybody here is pulling for me, and for the other dogs, too. Tucker says he would give his right arm—that is dangerous to say here—HA!—to take me home to Kentucky with him, but he will be happy if I can come home to you.

Tucker is going to write a letter to the training sarge at Fort Benning to let him know how I am doing. This week I'm a big hero because of two things that happened.

At the beginning of the week, we were on patrol when all of a sudden I got in Tucker's way and wouldn't let him go past me. The sarge wanted to keep moving, but Tucker told him I must know something to act so strange. A few more feet and Tucker and the others found a trip wire. They might have been blowed to kingdom come if I hadn't made Tucker stop.

Then yesterday, me and Tucker was leading a

patrol and come up on a couple hooches. I alerted.
Tucker told me I was a good boy, but when he tried to
move around me for a better look, I blocked his way
again. Tucker said now I had his attention. He told the
others not to go on, either. So instead of just walking up
to the hooches, our guys surrounded them and came in
real quiet. Then they hollered for the people to come out.
An old man and woman and a young woman with
kids came out. The sarge and two others went inside
and searched, and sure enough, in one hooch they found
a trapdoor in the floor. Three VC were hiding in there,
and were taken prisoners. They probably would have
shot up our patrol if our men hadn't sneaked up on
them.

Tucker and the others who were on those patrols
wondered how I do it. In the case of the wire, they
thought I could hear a breeze blowing over it. But they
can't figure out how I knew the men in those hooches
were the enemy. They think I'm the smartest guy
around. They come by at night, pet me, and tell me
thank you and they're glad I'm here. But they don't
want me to have to stay after they go home.

Tucker has been reading the books your mother sent.
He does a lesson a week in the grammar book. This week
he is working on "we saw," instead of "we seen." Last
week it was, "he did," instead of "he done." He has start-
ed to help the other guys speak better, but they don't take
to it much. The lootenant, who went to a fancy college,
told Tucker nothing would help him in life as much as
being able to talk good.

Tucker said to tell your mom he really liked Where
the Red Fern Grows. *He always loved his hounds, but*
they weren't as smart as Dan and Little Ann. He has

passed the book along to another guy to read.

Tucker had to go off by himself at the end of the book. He took me, of course. It took Tucker a long time to pull hisself—himself, I mean—together. He said it was the saddest book he had ever read and goes to show you how loyal dogs are. Dogs are willing to give their lives for you. Tucker wants to know what did you think of the book?

The drug situation here is going from worse to more worse. For a while, it was about half of the guys getting stoned. Now it's more. Tucker don't use. He's got three reasons not to. First, the men depend on him and me to be alert, and he would feel bad his whole life if somebody got hurt or killed because he was stoned. Second, he don't want to put me in danger. And third, he wants to go home. He saw somebody get wasted because he was out of his head and not paying attention.

Bigelow went home on Thursday. He was so nervous at the end he hung at the back of patrols for a couple weeks. When he left, he give me a present. He had carved my name on a metal strip in fancy letters. Tucker attached it to my harness and now I am the best-dressed dog in this part of the jungle. Also, I'm the only dog in this part of the jungle. HA!

Can you believe me and Tucker are coming up on five months here? It only seems like ten years. Seven months to go for Tucker. Keep working on getting me home. It's hell for dogs, even though you'd never know it because I smile all the time.

Tell Mom and Dad hi. Send Danny my best, and here's a big affekshunate lick for you.

Love,
Wolfie

21

I got a phone call from my congressman. Well, his assistant, actually—somebody named Terry. She said that Congressman Nelson had read my letters with interest (I'd sent four by then) and the newspaper clippings.

"The congressman has a good working relationship with people at the Pentagon and he is looking into the situation. He believes the way to put our country back together is by pulling together, which was his campaign slogan. He wants you to know how much he liked hearing from you.

"You call any time, Mark, that we can be of help to you. The people here in Colorado are the congressman's first concern. . . ." Blah, blah. You get the picture. The call didn't make me hopeful about getting real help. I thought I might call them back in a week or two to remind them how important I was to the congressman, but I didn't, because soon after that the roller coaster started up, and I was in the front car.

I came home from school one afternoon and wondered

186

why our old Chevy that Mom drove to work was sitting in the driveway. Then I figured out she probably got the afternoon off because she was going to have to work Saturday.

When I walked in, a quiet hung over things. The kitchen blinds, which Mom always opened when she got home, were shut, like eyelids.

"Mom?"

From the kitchen, I could see her sitting on the sofa, back to me, head tilted forward. I walked into the living room just far enough to see the crumpled tissues in her hand.

"No!" flew out of my mouth. I ran to my room and slammed the door behind me.

Mom ran down the hall after me. "It's not what you think." She tapped on the door. "Can I come in?"

She opened the door and put her head in. Her face looked made of wax, stiff and white. "Mark? It's bad news. But not terrible news."

"Danny or Wolfie?"

Mom slumped onto my bed like she couldn't support her weight anymore.

"Danny." Her teeth raked her bottom lip. She gulped a breath. "Wounded." She wadded up a piece of paper.

I put my arm around her shoulder.

"He was on patrol and stepped on a mine. He injured a foot and has burns on his leg and face. He's deaf, but they think that's temporary."

"Did he lose his foot?"

"Toes." She straightened out the paper. "I've been talking to the people at this number. A woman gave me all the details she had."

"Does Dad know?"

"I didn't want to call him at school and have him driv-

187

ing through traffic upset. I'll tell him when he gets here."

"Does Danny get to come home?"

"He was taken to a jungle infirmary. If the injury isn't too serious, they patch them up and send them back out. That probably won't be the case with Danny. If he requires surgery they can't do there, or if he gets an infection, they'll send him to a bigger hospital."

For a minute, I'd felt relief, but now that began to fade. Danny, the great dancer, crippled. Danny, the guitarist, maybe deaf. Danny, the life of the party . . .

Mom said we must be thankful. "When you think of the injuries he might have suffered. Families get telegrams, or officers appear on the porch with much . . . worse news." She said that over and over, a needle stuck in a groove.

When Dad got home, he asked Mom, "What are you doing home?"

"I came home early."

Dad looked in the refrigerator. Mom waited until he put vegetables from a plastic container onto a plate. Then he walked to the living room and his recliner. Mom let him sit down and pick up his paper before she sat down across from him, her fists balled.

"Randall, I have some upsetting news." She added quickly, "Danny is okay, but he's been hurt." She gave him the same details she'd given me, closing with the statement that many families got much worse news and we needed to be grateful.

She looked like her old self, scrunched into a ball on the sofa's edge, hands fidgeting, smoothing things over for Dad and me. She didn't look like the same person who had ordered people into line the day of my protest, and who had told Brother Rudy to use only our signs.

188

"You know our Danny. He'll be okay." Her voice was a tinkle. "If he isn't resilient, I just don't know who is."

Dad stared at his foot resting on the footstool like he had no idea how it got there. He didn't say anything. Then he got up, walked over to the phonograph, and put on *The Best of Mozart*. He sat down in the recliner again and gazed at the carpet. Mom sat across from him, hands working.

After a minute, she moved to the recliner, leaned over and hugged him. That kind of brought Dad back. He blinked, and put his arm around her.

* * *

"Mark!"

Mr. Sevorn hurried up the grocery store aisle toward me. "What's this about my Danny? Holy Mother of God, when I heard he'd been hurt, I dropped a carton of oranges all over the place. So, tell me all you know."

"Danny stepped—"

"Is it true he got hit by a mine? But he's okay?"

"He's—"

"They're sayin' it took off his foot. Is that right? Hey, they givin' him decent care? Marge has an uncle in the Pentagon. We'll make a call if we need to, and rattle some cages."

Mr. Sevorn thrust out his chin and peered into my face. We were about equal in height these days.

"I'd take somebody apart if Danny's not getting the care he needs. I'm sick about this, just sick." He shook his head. "Your brother used to dance when he was stockin'." Mr. Sevorn picked up an empty produce box, and sort of waltzed with it. "Like this, only, you know he was good. Or this . . ." Mr. Sevorn made a stab at some tap dancing

189

steps. "Another Sammy Davis, Jr., he was. He'd turn, and shuffle . . ." He made an awkward turn, trying to demonstrate. "He didn't care who was watchin', either. When it hit him to dance, he just broke out dancin'." Mr. Sevorn laid his hands on the bib of his white apron. "I can't bear to think of that kid not dancin'."

I stood beside the yellow onions, trying to remember what I had come in for. I didn't know how the news had traveled so fast, but then again, Danny had a thousand friends.

Our phone and house got overtaken by people wanting news about Danny. I didn't have the old jealous feelings about him being so popular. I only felt worried and sad.

I didn't go to school the next day. That evening, when the doorbell rang, I found Claire on the porch. She handed me my algebra and American history books.

"I thought you might need these." She glanced over her shoulder. Nathan and Peggy stood at the edge of the yard. Peggy lifted her hand in an uneasy wave.

Mom joined me at the door, and motioned for all of them to come in.

"We aren't going to come in," Peggy said. "We just wanted you to know we are very sorry, and if there's anything we can do . . ."

Dad came to see who was there and said, "Come in," in a grave voice. Everyone did.

Nathan shook Dad's hand. "I'm Nathan Richardson. We won't stay; we know this is a difficult time. I have two sons myself."

I got nervous when he said that. Dad might remember about Claire's brother in Canada. But Dad just said, "It's hard."

Nathan moved over and stood beside Dad.

Dad said, like they were having a private conversation, "I blame myself, partly. I encouraged him to go in."

"He might have gone without your encouragement. Boys have their own ideas."

"Maybe I should have urged him to go right to college. I keep thinking that."

I glanced at Mom. She was looking at the rug.

"We parents can't see the future when we advise our kids." Nathan looked sad when he said it. I had never thought about it before, but Claire's parents probably worried about their son, a long distance away in Canada and not able to come back to the States.

Peggy said, "You must feel so helpless."

Mom's lip trembled at that. "Helpless and far away. He's so young."

When Nathan and Peggy left, Nathan squeezed Dad's shoulder. "If we can help in any way, let us know. If you have to go out of town, Mark can stay with us. And we're available to keep an eye on your place."

At bedtime, Mom hugged me so hard she squeezed the breath from me.

"I thought of something today," I said.

"What?"

"This wouldn't have happened if a scout dog had been with Danny's patrol."

Mom nodded. "Remember how disappointed he was when the dog and handler they had left?" She sat on the edge of my bed picking pieces of lint off the bedspread and depositing them in her palm. She whispered, "God bless you, Wolfie."

* * *

Next day in first hour, Claire wrote me a note.

191

Dear Mark,

I'm so sorry about your brother. I want to talk to you after class.

Claire

She waited for me just outside the door. After we pulled away from the crowd moving down the hall, Claire took my hand. Mrs. Teesland, the skinny old prune who taught regular Algebra, walked past us, scowling. The school had a rule about public displays of affection. Claire looked right at Mrs. Teesland and kept firm hold of my hand.

At the art room, where Claire's next class was, she said in a quiet voice, "I know how you feel. You probably think I don't. But I have an older brother, too, and I know how I'd feel if he got hurt."

She couldn't know how I felt, because her brother was sitting it out in Canada, safe as a gopher in a hole, while Danny had risked his life. Somehow, I had lost sight of that during the past few weeks. Claire and her family might be nice people, but they stood up for a draft dodger.

"Say something, Mark."

I counted the lockers behind her. There were nine.

The first bell rang. "I gotta go."

I avoided looking Claire's way when I walked into American History. But I felt her eyes on me.

Mr. Casey handed back papers he had graded, and when he came to my desk he said in a low voice, "Mark. I heard about your brother. I'd like to hear more about it after school."

"I have to go right home," I lied.

When the bell rang, I made a beeline for the door. I don't know how she did it, but Claire beat me to it. The minute I stepped into the hall, she blocked my path.

192

"Mark." Her voice sounded firm, but her face looked ready to collapse. She took hold of my upper arm in a death grip and pulled me over near the lockers. "I want you to tell me about Danny."

"You know as much as I do."

"I don't know the details. Does he get to come home?"

"Maybe. We got a call this morning, and he has an infection in his foot. They're giving him antibiotics, but it's hard to keep things clean in the jungle hospital." I noticed I was short of breath. "They amputated three toes on his left foot."

"Does he need them for walking? Will he limp?"

"Don't know."

"Mark?"

"Yeah."

"You sound mad. Are you?"

I shrugged.

"Are you mad at the army?"

I shook my head.

"At me?"

"No." The word came out like a shot.

"What then?"

I stared past her. I wasn't mad, exactly. I just couldn't agree with people who thought like she did. We had to back the war. My brother Danny shouldn't lose body parts and maybe his hearing unless it was for a good cause. Dad had been right.

* * *

At school, I started to avoid Claire. After classes, I'd move to the center of the hall, where the shoving was worst, and disappear. I didn't know what I'd do if she wrote me more notes or called me at home, but she didn't. I'd see her from the corner of my eye, gliding down the hall with her friends, tall, regal, and sad.

For a few days after we got the news, Mom acted like the person we knew before Danny left and before she got a job. She made great suppers and put them in the refrigerator before she went to work. Dad and I didn't even have to make salads. When she got home, she whipped up favorite desserts for us before bedtime. She folded clothes and ironed like a maniac.

When the drain under the sink got clogged, Mom flitted around telling Dad, "I'm so sorry. You probably just wanted to relax tonight, and now there's this to contend with." You could tell Dad liked being fussed over. Those two looked like they were getting along a lot better.

Whenever the phone rang, we jumped. After school, I zipped home to check the mail. We were on pins and needles, waiting for more news about Danny. He was transferred to a hospital in Tokyo, and was taking antibiotics for the infection. It looked like he would lose his foot.

Suddenly, Mom changed again. Exactly one week after we'd gotten the news about Danny, she announced that she was going to do her part to bring an end to the war. She was joining a peace group called Mothers of Servicemen Against the Vietnam War.

"Don't you think that's a little disloyal to Danny?" I asked.

She turned and looked at me. "Explain."

"Danny put himself in danger for this country."

"No," she said. "Danny's country put him in danger."

"He joined; he wasn't drafted."

"It wasn't an informed choice. He was a kid influenced by ideas of patriotism and adventure. Other kids, like Tucker, had no choice."

"I wonder how Danny would feel about your group, if he knew." I said it with a hint of threat.

"He will, because I wrote and told him." She frowned. "If you think Danny supports the war, you need to reread his letters."

"He hardly mentions the war!"

"Exactly."

The night Mom went to her first meeting, she told Dad and me she wanted the dishes done and the counters clean when she got home. She marched out the door like she herself was going to war. Dad gazed after her, silent.

22

Mom called the army often to get updated reports on Danny.

It was up and down. We felt awful the day we found out they had amputated Danny's foot. But for a couple days after that, things looked good, like they wouldn't have to take any more of his leg. His hearing was coming back okay. Danny's fever went down and he seemed to be throwing off the infection. They thought they could replace his shattered bone with something artificial.

Then things got worse. Danny got a high fever. The surgery they tried on his leg didn't have the results they hoped for. They said the whole leg might have to come off.

Effie became a frequent visitor at our house again. She brought soup, rolls, flowers, and pots of tea. She insisted on dusting the furniture because "You have too many other things you must worry." I started dropping by her house after school, and we talked like in the old days. She wanted to know how my argument with the army was going. She had seen me on TV the day of the protest. "Can you think how proud I was?" She thumped her chest with the tips of her fingers.

Mr. Casey asked every day for an update. At first he asked in private, but so many people in class stopped by my desk to see how my brother was doing that Mr. Casey started asking at the beginning of the period, "Any news?" Even Dorweiller acted decent. He said he was sorry my brother had been hurt, and said it without a smirk.

I was glad that Wolfie was saving soldiers in Vietnam. But I worried about him more. Now that I knew how suddenly bad news could come, I jumped when the phone rang, and my hands shook when I checked the mail.

My feelings were all mixed up. One minute, I appreciated the good care the army was giving Danny. Next minute, I'd be crazy with rage because the army hadn't opened its eyes to how valuable the dogs were and given them the respect they deserved.

When people asked if Claire and I had broken up, I said, real casually, "We weren't ever going together." If somebody argued with that, I said, "She helped with the protest, but that was a while back." I wouldn't let myself look at her at school. Rick and I hung out in the halls, but the thing I had looked most forward to during school, talking with Claire, had disappeared.

One day when Mom made her routine call, she learned that the doctors had amputated Danny's leg at the knee. Rehabilitation would be easier, the person told Mom, than if they'd taken the whole leg. In another ten days, Danny would be returning home and would continue his therapy at the Denver veterans' hospital.

Wolfie sent a note telling Danny to get better. Tucker must have written the minute he got my letter because the response came so fast.

Dear Mark,

I am sorry to hear about my buddy Danny. Tucker says to tell you he is thinking about you all. Your Mom has been so good to him, like a second mother, and he knows she must be worried sick.

They pulled out a unit five miles from here as part of the plan to have the South Vietnamese soldiers take over more of the fighting. So Tucker and me hope we can watch our Ps and Qs and get out of this hot, muddy hell in another few months. Keep the pressure on the army about getting your good ole dog home.

You would think that with our troops going home, it would make everybody's attitude better. It don't. The morale here is in the toilet. A lot of guys become deserters. The others wonder why we're here and can't wait to get out. If you weren't a kid, I'd tell you some of the stuff that goes on. Well, I'll give you a hint. I wouldn't much want to be a officer. It can be dangerous for officers that the soldiers don't like. We heard of a case not far from here where a lootenant hit a booby trap that had been set by his own men. We got a good lootenant and I guess that's lucky for us and him.

In our unit, and most others at the front, race don't make no difference. But in some places, there is such bad blood between blacks and the whites that the troops are segregating theirselves.

Tucker got to talk with another dog handler the other day. It had been a long time since he'd got to visit with another guy who has a dog. Those two guys told stories and bragged on us for a hour. That guy was excited about the letters you are writing. He is crazy about his dog and says if the war is winding down, he ought to be able to take his dog out with him. But he's

scared that since his dog is young, like Wolfie, the army
won't give him up.
Tell Danny I send a nice big wet kiss.
Love,
Wolfie

I felt guilty after reading the letter. Tucker seemed to think I wrote letters all the time, but I hadn't written any since Danny got hurt. After the protest, Claire pushed me to write everyone that I'd written the first time, and I had. But when I didn't get much response, I lost some of my commitment. I had gotten one fairly encouraging letter from the army, but hadn't heard anything since.

So I pulled out that letter, reread it, then wrote the guy who'd sent it and asked what was going on with the committee that was looking into the dog policies. I reminded him how useful the dogs were, that Wolfie had saved lives and the army could repay that by sending him back to me after a year. I put in a word for the other dogs, too, that even if they belonged to the army, they shouldn't have to stay in Vietnam year after year.

I wondered who else I could write. I didn't have any bright ideas.

* * *

Effie went with us to the airport to pick up Danny. Mom insisted that she go along. Effie had said we needed adjustment time together as a family and Danny might not be ready to see anyone yet, but Mom wouldn't listen to her arguments. It was obvious Effie wanted to go, and I figured Danny would be glad to see her.

I was glad she was along on the drive because I felt so worried about seeing Danny that I didn't talk at all. Dad hardly said anything either. Mom chatted with Effie, and it wasn't all about Danny. They talked about some book that everyone was reading.

I think Mom was so relieved that her son would arrive home that she didn't worry about what it would be like to see a changed guy. I was afraid I would mess up—stare at his missing leg, or say something dumb. I could talk about sports, but I hadn't been following them much and guessed he hadn't either. Cars, girls, music—they all seemed like topics that could hurt Danny if I wasn't careful. I didn't even know how much I should ask about the incident when he got wounded.

* * *

Danny came off the plane in a wheelchair with a smiling stewardess pushing him. It was no problem not to stare at his leg. I couldn't take my eyes off his face. I tended to think of Danny as he looked in his senior picture—killer smile, lots of dark, curly hair. I'd seen the crew cut before, but it still startled me. But not as much as his face.

His cheeks were caved in like he hadn't eaten in weeks, and purple circles hung under his eyes. I'd known he would be changed, but somehow I'd imagined that the Danny smile would still be there. But his lower face had a grim tightness and his lips hung at the corners.

Next to me, Dad sucked in his breath.

I noticed other people looking at Danny. Sometimes when soldiers came home, people spat on them or insulted them. I was so scared someone might say something awful to Danny that my teeth were chattering.

Danny's injured leg, what was left, was propped up on the wheelchair. Danny looked around at the milling people, searching for us. Mom and Effie hurried forward, sort of knocking other people out of their way.

Mom should have gotten an Academy Award for her actions in the next few minutes. It was like she didn't even see that the army had sent back a different Danny, one you could hardly recognize. She leaned over and kissed him and said, "Danny! It's wonderful to see you." Her voice didn't jiggle even a little bit. "Honey, you look great."

Best Supporting Actress should have gone to Effie. She clasped her hands and her eyes got wide and happy. "Ya! Isn't he the handsomest thing?" She moved behind Danny's wheelchair, tilted her head at the stewardess, and said, "Now, I have the big disappointment to give. You cannot have him; he is ours. You must anuzzer prince find." She took the chair handles.

The stewardess came around and shook Danny's hand. "Good luck." She smiled at him, Mom, and especially Effie.

Dad and I had moved up to them by now. Dad leaned over and hugged Danny. He mumbled something, like "Welcome home," but it was hard to hear. I rubbed my shoe against my pant leg. Danny reached out his hand and said, "Mark. Hi."

I couldn't say anything then because I got too sad. Danny never called me Mark.

23

It could have been a good time, having Danny home again, hanging out with him, hearing stories, and having his noisy friends around. But it wasn't.

Danny hardly spoke to me, or anyone else either. The guys from the Invincible Tulip tried to get him to practice with them one night a week, but Danny turned them down.

Brad, the bass player, said, "We're not taking no for an answer. I'll pick you up on Friday, so be ready."

Danny shot him such a dark look, Brad's mouth clamped shut, and he didn't say any more about it.

Danny's flock of girl admirers, the ones who weren't at college, came around a lot the first few days. Karen, his former girlfriend, who was going to the University of Colorado, drove down to see him. The visits with the girls ended up like the ones with the guys. The girls chattered more, tried harder to pull Danny into conversation, and told him sweet lies, like that he looked great. But they got so little response, they quit coming around. Danny made it too hard for people.

Mom urged Danny to go with his friends when they invited him. "You're home now; you can do young-people activities again."

As soon as she said it, she knew she'd made a mistake.

Danny's brows knotted over his bony face. "But I'm not young."

Even though he wouldn't answer a single question about Vietnam from us or anyone else who visited, he insisted on watching the news. At 10:00 p.m. every night he wheeled himself into the living room and snapped on the TV. Pictures came on of soldiers in battle, body bags lined up on airstrips, and protests at home.

Danny would stare at the screen like he was in a trance. Watching Mom watch Danny was hard, too. She would curl and uncurl her fingers. When something particularly dramatic or controversial came on, her fingers would curl and uncurl almost in a blur.

U.S. negotiators were shown arriving for talks with the North Vietnamese or talks with the South Vietnamese. One day the report would be optimistic; the next day the reports said negotiations had broken down.

Dad was the only one of us who talked. Lectured, really, on the lessons that history taught. That a country needed to stand firm, that people needed to back their leaders. But it didn't have the ring it used to.

* * *

Mr. Casey was strolling around the room, checking kids' work. I wrote in big, scrawling letters:

There was a kid from the U.S.
Who saw that his country was a mess.
Old vets marched with flags,
Soldiers came home in bags,
And hippies made love for the press.

Mr. Casey, I saw, was heading my way. I made no attempt to hide the notebook.

"Is this history?" He pointed at my paper.

"Definitely."

He read over my shoulder. He let out a sigh. "You're right."

For a minute, I worried he wasn't going to tell me I needed to come in after school. Then he said, "But this isn't the assignment. Come see me after school."

When I got there, I started talking the minute I arrived. It seemed forever since I'd had Claire to talk to. Mom acted so fidgety and looked so tired, I hadn't talked with her, and I felt a little weird taking my troubles to Rick, considering what went on at his house.

"I'm worried all the time about Wolfie," I said.

"That's understandable," Mr. Casey said.

I told him about breaking up with Claire. I told him about Mom and the funny nervous habits she'd picked up. I told him about Danny and how far away he seemed.

"He gets this weird look, like he's in a daze."

"The thousand-yard stare. So, can anyone persuade him to get out and do things?"

"Dad takes him to the hospital on Saturdays for therapy. Sometimes, in the morning, Danny wheels himself to the window like he's interested in what's going on outside. We offer to take him out, but he says no. Dad thought if we planned an outing, Danny would like that. So on Sunday Dad said, "'Let's take a drive to the mountains and then stop at Baskin-Robbins.'"

"What did Danny say?"

"Danny said it sounded trivial. He sat in his room all day with the blinds closed. How was that so important?"

"Don't look for logic, Mark. Danny's probably not capable of it right now."

I stayed in Mr. Casey's room for an hour. At the end, I felt better enough to say something hopeful.

"Things can only go up from here, right? The song says the darkest hour is just before dawn."

Mr. Casey had a gloomy response. "We may see a great deal more darkness before any sign of dawn."

Something a bit encouraging did happen with Danny, however.

Effie had been coming over in the daytime, when the rest of us were gone, to sit with Danny. She brought him phenomenal things to eat, but he usually took only a couple bites and let whatever delicious thing was on his plate dry out while he went back to staring.

Effie didn't give up. She kept coming over with dazzling treats, and sat with Danny even though he didn't talk to her.

One day she said to him, "Danny, you must talk to someone about what you are thinking."

He said, "Spoken like an admirer of Freud."

"You did not die over there. But you could die here, from the terrible memories."

He didn't end up going to a psychologist, but he saw in the paper that a group of Vietnam veterans were meeting on Wednesday nights in a church basement on our side of town. Dad wanted to drive Danny over, but he turned Dad down. Said he wanted Mom to take him. When he came home, he had red eyes.

* * *

For a few days, the reports of peace got me so excited I almost forgot how dreary things were at home. The United States would be bringing more and more troops home and eventually pulling out altogether. Now when I passed the park, I pictured Wolfie and me in the near future—me tossing a shiny Frisbee and Wolfie spiraling into the air to catch it. Getting Wolfie home might even help Danny's outlook. No one had ever been able to resist Wolfie's cheerfulness.

The antiwar people must have been encouraged, too, because for a couple of days no reports of demonstrations or marches ran on the ten o'clock news. It might have been my imagination, but I thought Danny started to have more interest in food at dinnertime.

Then the situation took a bad turn. The United States had started bombing Cambodia. Critics of President Nixon said he was expanding the war even while he talked about peace. That brought protesters out in force—some of the biggest demonstrations yet.

We watched the ten o'clock news together one night, and I'll never forget it. When we turned it on, the screen showed kids running and screaming. In the middle of this scene, bodies lay on the ground. A riot had broken out during an antiwar demonstration at Kent State University in Ohio. National Guardsmen were called in. The guardsmen shot into the crowd and killed four college kids.

Mom dove for the TV and started to turn it off, but Danny ordered, "No!" So we watched the footage, over and over, of soldiers shooting into the crowd of kids, four of them crumbling, and everyone screaming.

That scene was horrible enough, but the one I'll never forget happened in our living room. Danny, who'd hardly said anything the whole time he'd been home, dropped his head and started to sob.

Mom, crying too, put her arm around his shoulder. Danny mumbled something I couldn't make it out. Mom said, "What, honey? What?"

"We're bleeding," he said. "Our country's bleeding."

Dad stared at a corner in the ceiling and moved his lips, having a talk with himself.

Danny said, "First they send us to the other end of the world to kill; now they're sending us to kill our own kids."

Mom went next door to get Effie because she thought Effie would take the news hard. Mom was right; Effie was terribly shaken.

"This happened in Germany," she said, with scared eyes. "Is very bad turn when soldiers start killing students."

Mom made a bed for Effie on the sofa so that Effie wouldn't be alone that night. While Dad and Mom got blankets and sheets, I went to the kitchen to use the phone.

Peggy answered.

"I'm sorry to call so late. Is Claire up?"

"Yes. We're watching the news." Peggy's voice wobbled. She called, "Claire? Phone." She asked, "How is Danny?"

"Better," I answered, thinking he might be much worse after tonight.

Claire came on. I said, "I'm sorry."

She didn't say anything.

"I've been a jerk. I've been awful."

"Yes." But I heard something in her voice that said she was glad to talk to me.

"Did you see the news?" she asked.

"Bad."

"Very bad." After a minute she said, "What are you going to do?"

"Wolfie, you mean?"

"Yeah."

It wasn't like I'd had any time to think about it. But I said, knowing it to be the truth, "I'm pulling out all the stops."

"What does that mean?"

"I'm getting him out of there."

"How?"

"You know how mad everybody is going to be now."

"Rioting is breaking out everywhere."

"People will be on my side. And on Wolfie's. I'm going to call the newspaper. Go on television. Get the Humane Society involved. Not the local humane association, the *national* one. I'll call Dave Hartwell and ask him to do another story. Buy a bus ticket and go to Washington and speak to Congress. Carry a sign outside the Pentagon."

"Mark?"

"Yeah?"

"Sic 'em."

24

"For what you want to get done, the mood of the country couldn't be more ripe," Mr. Casey told me. "Act fast."

I did. I called the *Denver Post* and the *Rocky Mountain News*. I had a little trouble getting to talk to a reporter at the *Denver Post*, but the first newsroom person I talked to at the *Rocky Mountain News* remembered my protest march and put me through to the features editor. Both papers set up interviews with me.

On TV, all kinds of governors and politicians—even some men in Nixon's own cabinet—talked about how outraged they were. Across the country, hundreds of universities and colleges shut down in protest. On campuses, students and antiwar groups turned out by the thousands to demonstrate. The Sunday paper ran a special section to print the flood of Letters to the Editor.

When I called our congressman, I had to redial dozens of times before I got through. His office was swamped with calls.

"I want to talk with Congressman Nelson himself," I said.

"That wouldn't be possible. I can give you to his assistant." The woman who answered the phone knew I was a kid.

"It has to be the congressman himself."

"The congressman is in Washington at a hearing and—"

"But you can get a message to him. Tell him to call me."

She sighed. "Give me your name and phone number." She only wanted to get rid of me.

"My name is Mark Cantrell. I have written the congressman several times—"

"Oh, yes. About the dog." The inflection in her voice changed to "How cute."

"—and I am seeing reporters at the *Denver Post* and the *Rocky Mountain News* in the next couple of days. I hope I don't have to tell them that the congressman won't answer my letters and calls."

"Will you be at this number for the next hour?"

"I will," I said.

He did call me back. He sounded less sure of himself than the times I'd seen him on television, or maybe he was just tired. It annoyed me that I had to explain the whole situation about Wolfie all over again, like it was new to him. But it did seem like he was taking notes as I talked because he had me repeat certain things, like the month when I sent Wolfie to the army, which unit Tucker was in, my age and the school I attended, and my parents' work phone numbers. When we hung up, he told me he would get back to me by the end of the week.

I asked, "Are you going to talk to the army?"

"Absolutely," he said.

* * *

The *Denver Post* reporter, a young woman with short red hair, set her camera bag on the sofa and sat herself in Dad's recliner. Mom was at work but had instructed me to offer the reporter cookies and tea. She accepted.

Danny wheeled himself into the living room, saw the reporter was there, backed up, and headed for the kitchen. The reporter, named Maggie, got up and followed him. Danny was trying to get through the doorway when Maggie stepped in front of him and introduced herself. Danny mumbled his name. She asked him if he would be available for a picture. He must have given her a look that would kill, because she blinked and came back to the living room.

Some of my old jealousy came back as I told Maggie about Wolfie and how he had saved soldiers' lives. She kept leaning over and looking past me to see if Danny was still in the kitchen. When I told Mom about it later, she said the reporter probably saw news value in including the story of my brother, who had just returned injured from Vietnam.

Though I thought she wasn't much paying attention and didn't take notes as I talked, when the paper came out on Sunday, the whole story as I gave it to her was there. She described Danny as having a "scowl as dark as his hair, which is outgrowing its military cut." Danny read the article, but, as with most things, had nothing to say about it.

* * *

In American History class on Monday, the class brainstormed ways I could expand my fight against the army.

After class, I held up my list to Claire. "Look at this. How can I do all this?"

She gave me that look of hers.

"What?"

"Mark." She pointed at the list. "How *can* you do all this?"

"Um, ask for help?"

"You think maybe Mr. Casey brought this up in class for a reason?"

"So that we would do some of this as a class project?"

She looked at me, blinking. Then she busted up laughing, her perfect teeth flashing.

* * *

For the first time since I'd said good-bye to Wolfie at the army base—maybe even before that, since Danny had shipped out to Vietnam—I felt like my real self. The body that woke in the morning and stretched, then crawled out of bed, belonged to me, and when I looked in the mirror to comb my hair, I knew who it was that looked back.

Danny started practicing at home with his crutches, ten minutes in the morning, ten minutes in the afternoon. It took a lot out of him and he sweated like a horse and needed a nap when he finished.

He talked to the people at the veterans' hospital and they scheduled him for a week of in-hospital physical therapy. He packed a bag, and Dad drove him there on Saturday.

* * *

The next Tuesday, one of the girls who worked in the school office walked into American History class and handed Mr. Casey a note. It ran through my head that it might be news for me. I'd been getting lots of calls since the *Denver Post* article. Also, I was waiting for word from the National Humane Society office in Washington, D.C. Then I had to smile. A little bit of fame was making me think every note in the world must be mine.

Mr. Casey read the paper, then said, "I'll be out of the room for a few minutes. Look over the quiz questions at the end of the chapter."

He walked up my row, bent at the waist, and said, "Mark, come with me."

Dorweiller bounced his eyebrows at me. "They caught up with you, dude."

I grinned.

As I followed Mr. Casey out, I let my imagination run. This might be more than a phone call. Maybe a TV crew was waiting in the hall. They'd call you out of class for something like that. Especially if the TV crew came from New York City.

At the end of the hall, Mr. Casey turned around. "Your mom is in the office, Mark."

I looked through the glass walls, and there she stood. She came across the carpet like a swan on a lake. Just that calm.

"Thanks for bringing Mark down," she said to Mr. Casey, who had moved behind me.

Some instinct told me not to look back at him.

I followed Mom out of the building like a chick follows a hen, matching the length of her steps all the way down the sidewalk.

"Get in," she said, which wasn't necessary, because I already had the car door open.

Something took over in me, and I knew things I

couldn't possibly have known. I knew not to ask, "Why are you picking me up in the middle of the day?" I knew not to make small talk or even look at Mom. I noticed from the corner of my eye that she drove with her hands folded around the wheel like it might try to fly off. Out the passenger window, I saw that the broken toys and old mattresses had been cleaned up from the yard where Agate had lived, and a sprinkler was going on the lawn. An old Asian woman I didn't know was walking up the sidewalk, pulling a dolly that held two sacks of groceries.

At the four-way stop, a guy in a purple car with dual exhausts had his radio turned loud. It was playing, "I-Feel-Like-I'm-Fixin'-to-Die Rag." The guy roared his engine and a stink drifted in through my window.

When we got into the house, Mom motioned me to the sofa, sat down next to me, and took my hands.

"Don't," I said.

She nodded.

"Dead?"

She nodded.

"How did you find out?"

"Congressman Nelson's office called me at work. He was investigating Wolfie's situation. When the army called him back, they told him the bad news."

"When did it happen?"

"Yesterday."

"I think I'd like to be by myself."

"Okay. I'll be downstairs. Call me if you need anything."

I went to my room and pulled out the sack that held Wolfie's old things. His fancy brush, his puppy collar, the toy I'd made from lake weeds, the leash, and the yellow sock toy. I laid them out on the rug one by one.

214

The phone rang a couple times. I thought it might be Dad. I knew he would be really nice and really sorry, but I couldn't risk having him tell me that I'd done the right thing.

When I looked at the clock, I saw that school had been out for a while. I went out on the front porch and was surprised to find the sky glittering blue and the sun beaming.

I started to walk to Claire's. But when I got to the intersection of Pine Street, instead of going straight, I took a left and headed for Rick's.

Rick opened the door.

"Your dad home?"

He shook his head and pulled me inside. He led me by my sleeve to his room. In the hallway, we met Greg. Rick gave him a black look and said between clenched teeth, "If you come in the bedroom, you'll die." Greg's eyes got huge and he nodded.

Rick shoved me onto Greg's bed and sat down opposite me.

I said, "Some day, it ought to be your turn. But . . ."

"Wolfie?" Rick asked.

I nodded. Tears started down my face. Rick laid his hand on my shoulder and said, "I'm sorry, buddy. I'm so sorry." When I looked up, he was crying too.

"All those letters for nothing," I said.

"All those letters for nothing," Rick said.

Rick left the room, slamming the door tight behind him, and returned a minute later with a stream of toilet paper. He tore it in two and gave half to me.

Rick and I sat a long time in silence. The next time he let go of my shoulder, he left the room to go talk to his mom. He must have told her not to call him for supper.

215

Then he came back and we sat on the beds across from each other, silent, until the room got dim. Rick turned on the lamp next to his bed. Greg never came in once; he didn't even try.

I appreciated that Rick didn't ask me how it happened. I didn't know, because I hadn't asked.

25

The letters from the guys who were with Wolfie on his last mission came in a big manila envelope, all but one. Tucker had put his in a separate white envelope.

It had been windy all week and overcast, but today the sky was blue and not a cloud was around, even above the mountains. The first day of summer vacation. I sat down on the porch to read the letters.

When I was sitting there, a robin pecking in the grass came really close, only a foot or so from my shoe. I tried not to move, and she stayed near for about ten minutes. Then she flew off with a worm dangling from her beak.

Danny came out to go around the block on his crutches, which he does a few times a day.

"Who are the letters from?" He eased down the steps.

"The guys in Wolfie's patrol."

Danny's eyes hung at half-mast.

"I hope"—his mouth worked—"you, that you . . ."
Danny had been trying to be a big brother to me during the last couple weeks, but it was like he couldn't find words, especially when he was stressed. Wolfie's death

had been hard on him because he was the one who suggested that I send Wolfie to the army.

"I'll be okay," I said.

There were nine letters from guys who had been with
Wolfie that day.

A guy named Dean wrote:

*I get jumpy when it starts to get dark here, because
night means danger. I used to call Wolfie over when I
was eating dinner. He would sit close and I'd hang my
arm over him. He didn't try to snitch off my plate, but
he did stare at every bite of food that went into my
mouth. I usually ended up sharing with him.*

*If a guy had a normal life, he wouldn't think it was
a big deal to hang his arm over a dog for a few minutes.
But those times with Wolfie were the only ones when I
didn't feel like the world had gone insane.*

I couldn't have read the letters the first week after I got
the news. Then, I didn't even want to know how he got
killed. Dad had called someone to find out what happened,
but I could only listen to a bit of the story. Knowing Wolfie
wasn't coming back was too much to swallow; I had to
take it in small bites.

I had holed up in my room. Mom got the school's rov-
ing teacher to bring me my assignments and give me tests,
but that was a waste of time. I didn't do the assignments,
and when I tried to do the tests, I couldn't make out even
the simplest questions.

Effie sat with me every day after Mom and Dad went
to work, like she'd done with Danny. That is, she sat in the
living room, and I lay on my bed in my room. When Effie
called me to the kitchen for lunch, I would be surprised,

either because it seemed like no time had passed or like years had. When Mom and Dad came home and came in to say hello, it was the same thing. Sometimes I thought they had come home early, sometimes it seemed like midnight.

A guy named Oliver sent this:

I don't want to speak bad of anyone, and don't get me wrong, Smalley's changed a lot. I wouldn't be writing this today if he and that dog hadn't done their job so good. But I didn't like Smalley much when he first got here. He thought he was the baddest guy around. He used to make something out of nothing. Even if you were just kidding around, he would ask how you meant it and if you thought you were better than him. He goaded guys into fights. (They made him put the dog away first.) Smalley was tough, I'll give you that.

But we all liked Wolfie from the first minute. Wolfie was Smalley's ticket into the group. On his own, Smalley might have stayed to himself, but with a big friendly dog at his side, he couldn't hardly do that.

I came to respect Smalley. He took great care of Wolfie, always fed and watered him before he fed himself. He told me once that he didn't let his mind wander for a minute when he was on patrol because his dog had been donated by a kid, and he wanted to make sure that kid— you—got your dog back.

Mom and Dad put together a scrapbook of Wolfie's life. They searched through boxes of pictures and dug out ones of Wolfie as a puppy, Wolfie with the neighbor's cat, Wolfie catching a Frisbee, Wolfie with Tucker in Vietnam. Mom sewed a beautiful cover for the scrapbook and Dad lettered all the captions in calligraphy. They included the newspaper clippings from the protest, and a tape of the Dave Hartwell program.

I liked this story from a guy named Bobbie.

Two guys were having an argument about something and it turned into a fistfight. One guy had the other one down and was punching him. The guy on the bottom was yelling and kicking and trying to throw the other guy off. All of a sudden everything came to a stop because of a terrible wail. When they looked over, Wolfie was stretched out on his side with his paw over his eyes. He was moaning.

The guy on the bottom said, "Look, you got the dog upset." They laughed and sort of forgot the fight.

A lieutenant named McClain wrote me a long letter about day-to-day life there and how it got better after Wolfie came. McClain said he'd been with a platoon before that had a dog and handler, and the other dog was loyal and smart, too, but Wolfie had something extra going for him.

His spirits never got down, no matter how bad things were. I remember once when biting insects were so bad, no spray helped. They were biting around Wolfie's eyes and he plunged into the river to get away from them. Once he was in the water, he started paddling and playing and begging the rest of us to come play. One by one, we gave up and jumped in, and for a few minutes we forgot we were in a steamy, dirty river in the sweltering, bug-infested boondocks.

There were days too miserable to bear. Wolfie could

tell when we needed extra cheering up, and on those days would go around and connect with every single man individually. He'd look you right in the eye, like you were the only person in the world. On a bad day when you could hardly make yourself care what happened to you, Wolfie managed to make you feel like you mattered. It was a small thing that was a big thing.

When I finished all the letters in the manila envelope, I read the one from Tucker.

Dear Mark,

    I wanted to tell you all about Wolfie's last hours on earth. It was a miserable day. There's any other kind here? Ha! It had rained all night, and the plants and underbrush were dripping. It was too hot to put on rain gear, so we just got wetter and wetter until our clothes were wringing. Wolfie's fur was soaked. The humidity was so high, there was no chance of drying out, even when we came out of the trees and the sun beat down on us.

    We was looking for a sniper or snipers. The lootenant said we had to find him before somebody else got killed. The sniper had killed somebody from our platoon a few days before. Men had been out on patrol, and me and Wolfie wasn't with them. The lootenant wouldn't send out any more patrols without the two of us.

    Everybody's mind was on a sniper who might be in a tree or behind one, and was straining to see if they could see or hear something.

    Wolfie alerted to something in the bushes. I put up my hand to tell the others to stop. They did. They knew Wolfie was on to something. I stared off into the trees,

221

thinking about that sniper, the other guys scanning the bushes. That's why no one except Wolfie saw Charlie stand up only a few feet from us and aim a gun at me.

Wolfie took a leap and sailed over the grass and knocked the guy over. He fired and shot Wolfie. That was the last shot he got off, because Simmons fired on him and got him.

It was crazy for him to attack from that close. Maybe others were around who were supposed to help, and got scared away when Wolfie attacked.

Wolfie was hardly breathing, but I insisted on getting him to a vet. We put him on a stretcher to carry him back to our camp. I was talking to him, but I don't know if he heard me. He never made a noise. From camp we were going to drive him to a veterinarian or a doctor. But Wolfie died in just a few minutes. I think he didn't have no pain, that he didn't know what hit him.

We carried him back and buried him in a clearing behind the tents. We covered the grave with rocks and plants and wrote WOLFIE on a cross with black shoe polish. The lootenant said words over him, a poem he knew from heart. A preacher couldn't have done no better.

Hardly nobody had supper that night. Some guys wrote letters, some smoked, some talked, some wanted to be left alone. It's not like we ain't seen death before, but I can tell you there was tears.

I feel like I lost a arm or a leg. I'm glad I'm alive but it don't seem right that I am and that brave dog ain't. I get up in the morning and reach for Wolfie, and the ground is empty.

Mama had sent a Bible with me and I'd hardly looked at it, but that night I stayed up late trying to

find a place that talked about dogs and heaven. The
lootenant showed me how to look things up in the index
in the back. I couldn't find one single thing about dogs
going to heaven. That makes me pretty mad at the
Bible, that it keeps its mouth shut on something so
important.

There's no way I can ever thank you enough for
sending that great dog. I loved him. There's no way on
earth I can apologize enough that he won't be coming
home to you.

Tucker

I read the letters many times in the next days. They made me so proud of Wolfie. Proud and sad and miserable.

26

May 1, 1975

Dear Wolfie,
  It's been a long time since I wrote you. Not like the first year after you died, when I wrote a lot. Mom must have collected the letters that I left beside the headstone Tucker sent. Someday, I'll ask for them.
  I came home Friday night for Dad's birthday party. Effie came over, and so did Danny. Danny has an apartment with two other Vietnam veterans. Claire couldn't come because she had to study for a test. Her school is three hours away from mine, so we only get together on weekends.
  You were on my mind a lot this weekend because of all the Vietnam coverage on TV. We huddled around the set, watching as the U.S. finished pulling out of South Vietnam. The North Vietnamese are moving on Saigon, so the U.S. evacuated the last of its personnel. Helicopters landed on the U.S. embassy roof, and people were scrambling to get on board. U.S. citi-

zens had first priority, then Vietnamese who had worked for the Americans. All kinds of other people wanted to escape, and marines with guns had to keep them back. At the airfield, flight crews could hardly get the doors shut on planes, and even after the engines started, Vietnamese men climbed onto the wings or grabbed the tires as the plane took off.

I feel sorry for President Ford, because he inherited a divided country. He took over when President Nixon resigned after the Watergate scandal. President Ford said that the war is officially over, and our government is calling it "peace with honor." But the scenes from Saigon look like chaos.

Our soldiers were pushing helicopters into the ocean and blowing up tanks so that the North Vietnamese can't have them. One bit of footage made us silent. It showed military dogs tied to their pens, barking and whining, while soldiers got into jeeps and drove off. A dog handler they interviewed said he was really mad because the military says dogs are equipment, and equipment must be left behind or destroyed. Some dogs were put to sleep; some are being turned loose. If they don't starve, they may get captured and eaten by the Vietnamese.

My hand is shaking, remembering how the dogs howled as the soldiers drove off. The Pentagon said that the World Health Organization wouldn't let dogs return to the U.S. because they were a disease hazard. But when reporters checked that out, the World Health Organization said that wasn't true. "Lied to again," the dog handler said.

That is the kind of story Claire wants to do when she becomes a reporter. She thinks she can get the truth *out of people, and knowing Claire, she's probably right. Mom thought because I like to write letters I might go into journalism. But I'm going to be a teacher, of either history or government. Dad thinks I'm following in his footsteps, but it was Mr. Casey who got me thinking about it, even though he didn't stay a teacher for long. He got in a lot of hot water after Kent State because he became so outspoken. Parents and kids stuck up for him with the school board and he could have kept his job, but by then he had decided to run for Congress against a guy who had supported the war. The press loved him—Mom said because he was handsome and passionate—and he came close to beating the incumbent. After that, he ran for mayor of the small town where he lives, and he won. He is in the news a lot for involving kids in town projects.*

Danny just left. It had to be a hard weekend for him with Vietnam in the news so much. We don't talk about Vietnam if he's around. I tried to give him a hug, but one of the things that has changed about Danny is that he forgot how to hug. "Keep the grades up, Marco Polo," he said.

Danny is active in Vietnam Veterans Against the War, especially on trying to get the army to recognize post-traumatic stress syndrome in soldiers. That's the name civilian psychologists have given to the psychological damage they see in Vietnam vets, but military psychologists don't believe there is such a thing.

Danny's prosthesis lets him do most everything he did before, even ski. But he is so involved with the veterans' group, he doesn't take time to play. It's like some shadow is chasing him and he is afraid to stop moving.

Danny had another project when he still lived at

226

home: Rick. When Rick and I got to be sophomores, Rick started running with a bad crowd and getting in trouble. When I tried to talk to him about it, he told me to butt out.

Danny saw that it was drugs. He started taking Rick out for pizza and movies. One day Danny came to pick up Rick at school and saw him with three guys in an alley. That was before he had his prosthesis, but Danny got out of the car and hobbled across the parking lot on his crutches, came up behind Rick, and knocked a joint out of his hand. He threw him against the building and screamed, "You want to end up like your dad?"

It scares us when we see temper like that in Danny. But the weird thing was, instead of hating Danny, Rick started to break with that crowd. By our junior year, he was back in basketball and hanging out with me. I hope Rick can come to college next year; this year he's helping his mom run the dry cleaning business.

The war's outcome was hard for Dad. He still believes it was right for us to be in Vietnam, but he hardly ever talks about it because the rest of us don't agree. Dad gets together with Nathan, Claire's dad, to play jazz. Claire says they are both worried about their oldest sons. Mike, Claire's brother, is homesick in Canada, but can't come back to the U.S. because he would be arrested.

Mom is head research librarian now. She loves helping school kids with projects. She helped Dirk, Claire's little brother, with a science project that went to nationals.

Effie still cleans her walk twice a day and now does ours, too, because Danny and I aren't here to do it. Mom says something has gone out of Effie since she

227

doesn't have boys to cook for. You should see the box of baked stuff I am taking back to school.

I sometimes get letters from the soldiers who wrote to me after you were killed, like Lt. Benny McClain. He keeps changing post office boxes, so I don't think he's doing too well. He loves to talk about you, though, and the impact you had on him.

Tucker and I write letters regularly. You should see how his spelling and grammar have improved. He is a college junior now and an A student, and wishing he could find a girl to marry. On Mother's Day, he calls Mom. Unlike Danny, he talks about the war. He doesn't think it was a mistake, but he's mad at how it was run. He thinks soldiers had to fight with their hands tied. He doesn't think less of Mom and Danny and me, though, that we ended up opposing the war.

I wish you could have come home. Today we would have gone to the park and played with the Frisbee. But I'm glad you died being a friend, instead of being abandoned like the dogs we saw on TV. I couldn't have stood that.

I worried from the beginning that I'd made a mistake by sending you, and when you got killed, I blamed myself. Effie was a big help to me then. She said a lot of boys came home to their families because of you. "You did a good thing," she told me.

Effie doesn't think like Mr. Casey. She doesn't trust governments to make things better for people. You can see why she would feel that way, having lived in Nazi Germany. Mom and Danny don't put much trust in government either, but they believe in groups—that people can band together to make changes. I kind of hold with that idea, but Effie doesn't. She believes it's

228

up to individuals—that a man or woman must choose to be personally good. That is the way to a good life, she says.

If she's right about that, you had a great life. Not just by dying to save someone, but by the way you acted every day—friendly with everybody, and enjoying yourself so much that those around you had to feel better.

I don't feel anywhere close to knowing how to do that. Some of the guys on my floor are so annoying, I wouldn't give up my place in line for them, let alone try to make their lives better. I told Effie that one day, and she got her wide-eyed look and said, "Mark! Of course it is difficult! We are mere humans. We have not the great gift of dogs. To the human was the big brain given, but to the dog went the large, loving heart."

Some people would laugh at this ambition—to be so decent as a person that I'd rank up there with a good dog. I don't know if anyone can be that good. But Mr. Casey said we have to stand on our tiptoes to reach the dreams on the top shelf.

It's six o'clock, and I need to head back to school. Don't think I've forgotten you. I never will.

Love,
Mark

Author's Note

Although this story is fictional, dogs did serve heroically in the Vietnam conflict. Some were donated by civilians like Mark. Dogs have been credited with saving more than 10,000 soldiers' lives in Vietnam. Scout dogs like Wolfie, and their handlers, had a particularly dangerous job, walking point at the front of patrols, searching for hidden dangers.

Approximately 4,000 dogs served in Vietnam. Of that number, an estimated 500 were killed in action, and disease claimed another 600. Only 200 dogs made it out of the country, but none of them returned to civilian life. The military classified dogs that were sent to Vietnam as "equipment." When the U.S. pulled out of Vietnam, equipment was left behind, and that included the dogs. Some dogs were euthanized, some were transferred to the South Vietnamese army, some were simply abandoned.

Vietnam was not the first war in which the United States army used dogs. Following World War II, however, dog soldiers received honorable discharges and came back to the United States to live out their lives in peace, often with the families who had donated them to the military, or sometimes with their handlers.

Over the years, veterans, former dog handlers, and sympathizers have struggled to establish memorials in honor of the dogs that served in the military. Today, memorial sites exist in New York, Georgia, California, Tennessee, Texas, and Guam.

In November 2000, President Clinton signed into law

the Military War Dog Resolution, which stopped the practice of euthanizing military working dogs at the end of their service. Retired dogs now can be adopted by law enforcement agencies, former dog handlers, and other people capable of caring for the dogs. As of this date, legislation to establish a national war dog memorial site in Washington, D.C., is pending.